ONE SINFUL NIGHT

BY

STACEY KENNEDY

Featuring...

Shadowed Soul
Forever Bound
Takedown
Somewhere in Between
All She Wants for Christmas is Her Dom

Decadent Publishing Company
www.decadentpublishing.com

One Sinful Night
Copyright 2012 by Stacey Kennedy
ISBN: 978-1-61333-166-8
Cover design by Fiona Jayde and Cribley Designs

Published by Decadent Publishing Company
www.decadentpublishing.com

Printed in the United States of America

SHADOWED SOUL

BY

STACEY KENNEDY

CHAPTER ONE

Broken heart. Endless tears. Ellie was sick of mourning the loss of her last asshole boyfriend, Gerrid, who stomped on her heart because the word *faithful* didn't hold any meaning in his vocabulary.

"All you need to do is purr and you're a total sex kitten," Kenna said. "That date of yours is going to get a hard-on the second he sees you."

Her best friend was smokin' herself. With her blue eyes and blonde hair—dressed in a short, plaid shirt and white blouse tied up to show her mid-section, she looked like a typical Barbie. "A school girl?"

"Don't knock it," Kenna retorted. "This outfit has gotten me laid a few times over."

Commitment never appealed to Kenna, but she wasn't a slut either. More of a playgirl_she loved the benefits of the single life and lived it to the fullest. Ellie tried to think the same way. Once she'd loved and loved hard. Now, she'd given up on the idea and hoped to walk in Kenna's shoes. "You ready to go?"

Kenna grabbed onto her own breasts and squeezed them.

"Ready."

Ellie headed to the front door, laughing. She owned the luxurious condo not because of her job at *Transatlantic Bank* as a financial advisor. It paid well enough, but she purchased the house from the funds of her father's estate five years ago.

At the front door, she stepped outside and the steamy Miami summer night caused her skin to flush. A month ago, she'd enlisted the services of Madame Eve, who owned the matchmaking service 1Night Stand. She didn't want to find the man of her dreams, simply wanted a one-night stand to leave a lasting impression on her body.

After locking the door, she glanced over at Kenna. "Thanks for coming along—I might be after some action, but in case he's a creep, you're my escape route."

Kenna chuckled. "Look at you, Miss Nympho."

"I just need something to make myself feel better. I'm sick of being in the dumps."

Kenna wiggled her eyebrows. "What you need is a hard reminder there's plenty of good still left in the world."

"A big, hard reminder, eh?"

Kenna nodded, grinning from ear-to-ear. "An oversized one, hopefully."

Falling into stride with her friend, she walked briskly down the street. The sooner she got to the bar, the sooner she could get her groove on. She longed to get away from the ache in her chest and nothing she had tried so far worked. A one-night stand had to make her happy, even if for a little while.

As they arrived at Nocturnal Nightclub, the downtown core boomed with energy. She received a few glares from middle-aged people for her choice in attire, which confirmed she'd chosen correctly. The leather dress hugged her in every way it should. Low enough to show off her breasts, making them swell at the top, and the hem rested just below her ass.

The bright lights outlining the large, square building illuminated the dark sky. The bass from the music inside vibrated against her skin. A line of people stood alongside the building awaiting entrance.

"Dammit, we're going to have to wait to get in." She desperately wanted to meet her date, not stand outside for half the night. Her hair would frizz and by the time she went in, she'd appear more tired than sexy.

Kenna grinned. "Here's where my strategy comes into play."

"What strategy?"

"*Do* men who guard the door so you don't have to wait." Kenna strode up to the bouncer, not at all put off by the scowls she received from the crowd. The mountain of a man leaned down to kiss her cheek.

These two had definitely heated up the sheets, and judging by the smolder in his expression, he still wanted her. Kenna always could cause that effect. She kept the men in her life lusting after her with their tongues wagging out. They never appeared to harbor ill feelings. Most of the time, she gathered men who'd do anything for her.

Ellie envied that about her.

After a short conversation with the bouncer, Kenna glanced over her shoulder and waved her forward.

Offering an apologetic glance to the crowd for butting in line, Ellie entered the establishment heading straight for the second floor. She surveyed the lower level of the bar from the landing. Loud, thumping beats blasted through the large space and people filled the dance floor.

"He's supposed to meet me on the third floor," she called out over the music.

Kenna nodded, snatching up her hand and hurried up the

remaining stairs. As Ellie entered the rooftop bar, warm air wrapped around her, and the fresh summer scents mixed with exhaust from cars and ocean greeted her.

Much like the other floors, bartenders were scattered around to serve alcohol, tables with chairs placed throughout, and the dance floor was stuffed full of intoxicated people. The views of Miami were a spectacular sight with miles of skyline lighting up the dark sky.

Kenna stopped at the one of the bars, leaned over the counter, and squeezed her breasts together so they swelled out the top of her shirt. "This will grab his attention."

The bartender came to her side in two-point-two seconds. His dark, styled hair swept over his eyebrows as his baby blues focused on her alone. "What can I get for you?" he asked her tits.

Kenna squished the girls together with her arms and the man licked his lips. "Two Funky Cosmos and four shots of sambuca."

He finally looked into her eyes, nodded, and hurried off to prepare the drinks.

Ellie chuckled. "I'm surprised he didn't bury his head in your cleavage."

"Oh you laugh, but just wait." Kenna smiled at the bartender who presently overfilled the shots, spilling the dark liquid onto the wood. His eyes widened at the alcohol dripping from his fingers and he fumbled to clean up the mess.

When the server returned, Ellie downed a shot in haste. By the time she finished off the second one, he'd placed a Funky Cosmo in front of her. "On the house, ladies."

"Thank you." Kenna swiped the sugar off the martini glass with her tongue in an undeniably sultry gesture.

He groaned.

Ellie sipped her drink to refrain from laughing. To be so bold needed confidence. She had to pay closer attention and learn a thing or two from Kenna.

"Stick around for the night and I'll quench that thirst of yours." His voice deepened and a grin quirked up the side of his mouth.

"Mmm..." Kenna hummed, "I am quite thirsty."

Barf.

With a wink, the bartender ventured off to serve other customers. Ellie huffed. "You cannot be serious? The first guy you talk to is already chasing after you."

Kenna fanned herself. "I have a gift." She swallowed a big gulp of the martini. "What about your date? Do you see him—and stop being so nervous."

"No, I don't and I *am* nervous."

"Oh, please." Kenna dismissed the remark with a wave of her hand. "Like any guy wouldn't dream of taking you home. So stop it."

If only Ellie believed that. She scanned the dance floor, searching for the man matching the picture Madame Eve had emailed her. Instead, she got a few heated glances from guys she wouldn't touch on her worst days. So, instead of continuing to search, she lingered taking a seat upon a stool, listening to the bartender and Kenna talk dirty nothings to each other. *Why isn't he here?*

After she downed her second Cosmo, goose bumps pimpled on the back of her neck, and she glanced over her shoulder to discover her date standing against the back wall. His gaze focused on one person, her.

Hallelujah!

"Oooo...my night is looking up," she exclaimed.

Kenna didn't respond, too busy playing googly eyes with the bartender. Ellie jabbed an elbow into her side. She hissed as she rubbed her ribs. "Ow, what?"

"He's here. I'm going to dance." She gestured behind her and grinned to show her intentions.

Kenna peeked over her shoulder before focusing back on Ellie and giving a shit-eating grin. "Have fun."

Ellie slid off the stool, keeping her focus on the stranger. His mere presence screamed sex. Much taller than her five-foot-five frame—around six-two—but built like a brick shit house. His muscular arms were crossed over his chest, his broad shoulders tempting her, and she couldn't wait to run her hands over them tonight.

Putting a little oomph into her step, she made her way onto the dance floor. The loud techno song washed over her, and the vibrations were strong against her feet. Her kinda music—hard and dirty.

Staying at the edge of the crowd, she found her beat and moved with the rhythm. Twirling, she ran her hands along her torso and did anything and everything to gain his attention.

To all appearances, her plan worked.

He dropped his arms to his side and stepped forward. His sparkling blue eyes, short, fashionably-styled black hair, and chiseled features warmed her right down to her toes. Her heart raced. Her insecurities drifted away. The world around her ceased to exist, leaving only him and her.

Wetness pooled in her panties. His nostrils flared and his heated gaze burned deeper. He approached and as he settled in front of her, he grabbed her lower back and yanked her against his hard body. Her head tilted back and he leaned down, cupped her nape, and kissed her.

A kiss not meant for strangers_not meant as a sweet hello. No, a promise he would pleasure her and she sang a big *thank you, Jesus* for bringing him to her. No thoughts. No regrets. Just two sweaty bodies going at it until exhaustion set in.

♎

Bryce had spotted the woman Madame Eve had set him up with the moment she stepped onto the patio. His interest, though, had nothing to do with her beauty. Not that her appearance didn't please him—her firm, yet curvy body was made for his attention. Her breasts bounced with each step she made and he yearned to lick the swell of them. Her long, flowing blonde hair reached down to her spectacular ass, and he imagined what she'd looked like naked with those locks decorating her skin.

Again, not what captivated him. Nor was he interested in the fact that she accepted his kiss without a word spoken. An easy lay. Although the thought did appeal to him, and he planned on finding a home between her thighs, the pain in her expression held his focus. Her soul was shadowed.

He'd grown tired sixty years back of the same old lifestyle. Having a human consort held no interest for him any longer. After he'd been given immortality, the endless women and spectacular nights of sex satisfied him. Not any longer. He demanded more—to stop taking and give something back in return.

These past years had altered his life in a remarkable way, and Madame Eve's services assisted him in finding broken women. He requested a match who wasn't in search of love, but who was coming off a broken heart and needed to gain back her confidence. Madame Eve never failed him.

With his mouth slanted over hers, he didn't doubt his indulgence. Her lips were wet and she followed his movements eagerly. Each swirl of his tongue made her sink further against him. He pushed his hard cock against her stomach to show her his enthusiasm.

Her soft whimper would fall on deaf ears in the loud club, but the lovely harsh breath sounded, crisp and clear, to him. He yearned to feel her around his cock, to make those noises shift into rumbles of pleasure.

After a final butterfly kiss, he backed away but caged her face in his hands. He could get lost in the smoldering green eyes staring back at him. "You taste spectacular."

"Um...." Her innocent smile tightened his cock. She had no idea how breathtaking he found her. "I've never been described quite that way before."

Wicked thoughts played on his mind. If her mouth tasted so divine, he could hardly wait to sink his teeth into her neck and feast on her delectable flavor.

Four days had passed since his last feeding and his hunger demanded to be sated. The woman he held in his embrace could be the perfect way to satisfy his cravings. Her kisses came greedy, her willingness showed, and he could hardly wait to get her home.

Blood was his survival. For years, he'd been alone, and his only choice was to feed in this manner. Once, true love had found him. However, the night she learned of his heritage, she ran in fear. His heart died that night and never returned. "We...er...haven't introduced ourselves except for the profiles Madame Eve sent." Her cheeks burned crimson. "I'm Ellie. You are?"

He grinned at her stumble. "Bryce."

"I'd say it's nice to meet you, but I think we've already covered that."

"Indeed we have."

She smiled sweetly and the kindness gave him a sense of not

being a night creature. "Would you care for a drink?"

"Sure," she replied. "A Funky Cosmo."

He slid his hand into hers, threading his fingers against her warm skin and she gasped. So responsive. So sensitive. Pure fun. He led her away from the dance floor toward a table off in a corner. He pulled out her chair and she lowered down into the seat, crossing her legs. Her skin was creamy and smooth. He vowed that by the end of the night, his tongue would run the length of those spectacular calves.

"Stay here," he told her. "I'll be right back."

She nodded, bouncing her leg across her knee. If she sought to tease him—her ploy worked.

He left to fetch her beverage and returned to the table a short time later. He set the martini in front of her and she cocked her head. "You're not a drinker?"

He shook his head, sitting across from her. "Not alcohol, anyway."

"Too bad." She raised the glass to her mouth and took a long sip. "It's good."

He contained his amusement. Liquid bravery and apparently, she needed oodles of it since she consumed nearly half of her Cosmo in one gulp. "So, Ellie, tell me why you arranged to meet me?"

"Well...I...." She hesitated, guzzled her drink before she placed the glass on the table. "I'm looking for a night of fun."

"You want to fuck?"

Her eyes widened before she laughed nervously. "Isn't that why you signed up with Madame Eve, too?"

"It's not the only reason, but fucking you doesn't sound like a bad way to spend a night."

"No, not a bad night at all." Her voice came out in the softest of whispers, and she studied the floor.

He ran his finger up the outer part of her calf. "Before we proceed with our evening, tell me who broke your heart?"

Her head jerked up. "Pardon?"

"Explain why I see so much heartache in your expression."

Her breath left her lungs in a loud whoosh. "Why do you care?"

"It interests me."

She stared at him with a mask of suspicion. "What's going on here? I told Madame Eve not to mention that to anyone." She stood in a huff. "I'm not interested in being someone's pity fuck." Turning to the side, she sought an escape.

He latched onto her wrist. "Madame Eve never told me about your recent breakup. I see deep pain behind those pretty eyes of yours, and to give you the night of pleasure I intend to, I have to hear what happened. So, please indulge me."

Her mouth formed an O. Either his question stunned her or she believed him, since she settled back into her seat. "There's not much to tell you. I wasted three years of my life on someone who didn't deserve my time."

"Didn't deserve *you*," he corrected.

She snorted. "However you say it, it's still the same. Long story short, he cheated and I dumped him on his sorry ass."

Her cold tone didn't fool him for a second; the event affected her more than she let on. "But his cheating still saddens you?"

"No," she snapped. At his arched eyebrow, she sighed. "Okay, well, maybe a little. I guess I should've seen it coming. Gerrid's a jock, always needs to be a winner. Obviously, I didn't make him feel special enough, so he looked elsewhere."

He ran his finger across her jawline. "Any man who doesn't see you as a prize is a fool."

She smiled, which held no strength. "Of course you'll say that; it's a sure way to get yourself laid."

He arched his eyebrow again. "I'm getting laid regardless of what I say, am I not?"

"I...oh...."

He would have let her continue since he found her mumbled speech endearing. But he yearned to bring the strong woman inside of her out. "The man is no longer in your life?"

She nodded, firm and determined. "He is."

"If you could return to him, would you?"

She pondered. "I'd only return to be the person I was when I first met him."

Her answer didn't unravel his confusion, but his curiosity couldn't be withheld. "So, you're not in love with him anymore?"

She snorted. "How do you care for someone who has hurt you so bad? No, I don't have feelings for him anymore. Do I miss the man I fell in love with? Yes, but Gerrid's not the person I once knew."

Her awareness intrigued him. "Who is he then?"

"A man who desired more than I could give him." Her chin quivered, but with a long breath in, she composed herself. "My Gerrid made me feel like only I existed in the world."

"And you think you can't ever experience such things again?"

Her intense stare never faltered. "I've realized it's impossible. Love is about what you need at that time. I made him happy then, but people change and grow. Do I think it's possible to grow together?" She shook her head. "No, I can't believe in that."

"So, you think he cheated on you because you both changed?"

She shrugged. "A question you would have to ask him. I can't tell you why he no longer saw me as someone who made him happy."

The honesty she offered blindsided him. She spoke the truth

so freely, regardless of the fact she had no reason to put such faith in him. But one thing she said couldn't be ignored. "Explain to me what you meant by it's not him you miss, but yourself?"

"I want to be the woman I once was. The one who was filled with such happiness I thought I might explode." She bowed her head to her hands and sighed, so deep, before she looked back at him. "I once believed in fairytales. I didn't know the feeling of a broken heart, hadn't seen the world with cynical eyes, and that's what I miss. The old me."

His heart bled for her. He'd spoken to many women before her who'd spun a similar tale and none had ever given him the response she had. Usually, he heard, "fuck the cheating scumbag," but they never expressed what had been stolen from their lives. The truth of her words, plus the raw agony in her eyes, gripped him in the worst way. He cupped her cheek. "Do you believe you'll ever find the woman you once were?"

She leaned against his touch. "You can't go back and get something that's gone."

"Yet, you hide nothing of yourself," he offered. "Doesn't that declare the naïve part of you remains?"

"No, it means I have nothing to hide. You either like what you see or you don't."

He ran his thumb over her bottom lip. "I'm impressed by what I see. I appreciate you sharing your story with me, and I'm intrigued to learn more about you, but I'd much rather learn these things from you by the way you moan."

"Enough said." She snatched up his hand, holding it tight, and after a wave to her friend, she dragged him from the club.

He allowed her to pull him with her. She might be intent on lifting her pain, attesting she needed to be something different, but he would prove her wrong. She only needed to be herself.

Chapter Two

The black Porsche was parked right outside the club's entrance. Ellie couldn't appreciate the car's worth—she knew zilch about them—but it looked pretty and expensive. Her interest held more in the man opening the passenger door.

Hadn't she learned the lesson growing up? *Never talk to strangers and don't go anywhere with them alone.* He opened the door and gestured for her to get in. The question lingered in the air. *Can I go through with this?*

He grinned, sultry, causing her body to warm in intimate places.

Yes, I can.

She sank into the leather seat and inhaled the new car smell, studying Bryce as he approached the driver's side door. Her heart pounded at the thought of the night of lust ahead. He settled in beside her and in a move that stunned her and seemed impossibly fast, he pulled her toward him and pressed his lips against hers. His kiss consumed her. Tongues slid in a wicked embrace as lips crushed together. Goodness, the man could kiss.

Her clit pulsed and the wetness along her panties made her squirm. He chuckled, low and deep, leaving her panting. "Don't worry. I don't live far." He slammed the car into first gear and gunned it down the street.

She dropped her head back and breathed deep to settle herself. Closing her eyes, she heard the hum of the engine, but as cold fingers caressed her leg, she gasped. Peeking sideways at him, she found him grinning, but he kept his focus on the road.

He trailed his touch along her inner thigh. "Open up for me."

It didn't sound like a question, more like an order. One she didn't intend to refuse. She spread her legs, desperate to feel the chill of his touch against her moist heat. "Can't wait, can you?"

"I refuse to wait." He ran his fingers over her lace panties. She should've been embarrassed by how damp she made the material, but couldn't find it in herself to care.

"Mmm...." he droned, circling her clitoris. "Apparently, I'm not the only one who is eager."

The purr of his voice intensified her arousal and she swirled her hips. "Just ready," she countered.

He pulled the thin fabric to the side, exposing her sensitive flesh, and stroked her slick folds. "I'd say you're fervent and then some."

Nothing else existed; only the feeling of him teasing her dampened flesh. Each caress he made burned wicked in her body. Something she'd never experienced before. Gerrid only played with her as preparation, so he could pleasure himself. This, however, was a world apart from that. The way he worked his finger against her clit had nothing to do with him and was all about her.

Just as the hint of an orgasm rose, a mouth joined hers. She opened her eyes to realize he'd stopped the car. He yanked her over the stick shift and onto his lap, continuing to dance his lips in tune with hers.

He opened the car door, and with her wrapped around him, he exited. Tearing her mouth from his, she heard the ocean waves crash along the shore and discovered that his home was situated on the beachfront.

"The night is perfect," he said, drawing her focus back to him. "Look above you."

Up in the sky, the full moon shone in splendid glory. "Pretty."

"Indeed you are."

She gazed upon him and a grin turned up the corners of his mouth. Her cheeks warmed. "Thank you."

Surprising her, he didn't carry her toward the house. Though, calling it a house might have been an understatement. The modern mansion constructed of gleaming glass amazed her. "You live here?"

He chuckled. "Do you approve?"

"Ah, yes, I'd say I do."

His eyes twinkled with a flash of emotion she couldn't quite place, but when he squeezed her ass, she decided she didn't much care. "I thought you might enjoy the view out back."

She peeked over her shoulder and wriggled out of his hold. Lush, green, tropical trees surrounded the expansive back yard with a pool designed as an exact replica of an Amazon rain forest lagoon in the center. Along the back fence, a waterfall splashed between deep green mossy stones and the plant life. The decorative lights scattered around the yard gave off a romantic glow.

Was she dreaming? Everything seemed too perfect. Before she had time to consider it further, he closed the distance between them and captured her in a kiss that tickled right down to her sensitive flesh.

After a nibble on her bottom lip, he backed away. "You up for a soak?"

"Am I ever."

He gave her a once over and clenched his jaw before he approached a chair off to the left side of the lagoon. "Remove your clothes and get in."

Did I hear him right? "You're not joining me?"

He shook his head.

She tried to figure out the reasons behind his decisions, but failed. "Why?"

"Is it so hard to believe I'm more interested in watching you?"

"Well...er...yeah."

He said nothing, which irritated her. Shouldn't he be trying to woo her? It'd been one thing to gather the courage for a one-night stand. But to expose herself to a perfect stranger while he observed her—that would take confidence she didn't have.

After a pause, his eyebrows arched. "Have you changed your mind about tonight?"

Have I? Her present predicament was something she'd ever faced before, and she doubted she'd experience again. She didn't want to look back and say, *you should've done it.* For all the misery she'd experienced the past few months, she needed to step out of herself, dare to be brave, and find her poise again. Instead of answering him with words, she reached to the first button on her leather dress, opened it, and continued, one by one. His gaze followed her fingers until the garment pooled at her feet.

"Do a little turn. Let me admire you," he murmured.

She slowly spun around. "Do you like what you see?"

His grin said more than words could have. "I love what I see." He inclined his head toward the water. "Go get wet."

"I already am."

His eyes twinkled with amusement. "Ahh...I thought as much, but we both know that's not what I meant."

Sliding off her thong panties, she tossed them aside, pleased to hear a deep groan behind her. She stepped down the stone stairs. Pushing off, she swam and twirled, allowing the warm water to glide along her body. Minutes passed as she simply enjoyed the pool, forgetting everything and just being in the moment.

Bryce squatted at the edge. "All done?" He reached for her.

"That was wonderful." She slid her hand into his and he pulled her up out of the water. The chair he'd been sitting in was now positioned off to the side facing a big boulder surrounded by lights. How had he moved the chair so fast?

He tucked his finger under her chin, breaking into her thoughts. Leaning in, he pressed his lips against the hollow of her neck and she shivered. Each swipe of his tongue, graze of his teeth, made her burn. Her breathing deepened and she tilted her head to the side in a plea for more.

"You like me here," he whispered.

"Yes." She exhaled. "I don't know why, but yes, I love you touching me there."

He butterfly kissed her nape before backing away and gestured toward the rock. "Go and take a seat."

Ellie studied the area, the chair, and the implication became clear. A stage had been set. "You want me on there?"

"My home is secluded; only you and I are here."

"I'm up for some fun," she retorted. "But how can I be sure you aren't taping me and I'll end up on some amateur porn video site?"

His eyelids lowered and a burn filled their depths. "Because I never share." His head cocked. "Do you believe what I say to be the truth?"

To trust a stranger seemed absurd, but she held no doubt he was being honest with her. "I do."

"That's a good thing." He smiled. "We haven't discussed what will take place here, but did you have preconceived notions about how this would play out?"

"Well...." she paused. "I thought we would just, you know, fuck."

He ran his finger along her neck and down to the swell of her breasts. "I plan to do so, but first, indulge me by allowing me to watch you."

She stood frozen in place. Yes, she wanted to be different, stronger, a new Ellie, but she'd never been displayed in this manner. "I don't want to refuse you, but—"

He placed a finger over her lips to hush her. She stared at him, silent, wondering what in the hell would happen next.

$$\mathcal{L}$$

Before Bryce took her—and he planned to drive into her moist heat until she screamed his name—he planned to show Ellie she could do things she never thought herself capable of doing and force her to see the strength she sought already lived inside her.

She stared innocently at him, but his focus couldn't remain on her face. Her nipples were erect and ready for his attention. Overwhelmed by her creamy skin and succulent curves, he hungered for a taste of her.

He ran his hands down her arms. "You're so lovely." Beneath his touch, she trembled. Her lips parted and she sighed. "I'm fighting against myself not to take you right here." He trailed his touch across her shoulders moving, down to her breasts.

"Why are you waiting?" She exhaled.

With his cock straining in his pants, why *didn't* he bend her over and take her 'til she shuddered around him? His sense of purpose held more strength than his erection. He couldn't help her if he satisfied her lust—he'd only ease the ache between her thighs. After a lazy swirl of his finger on her nipple, he decided to answer her question. "It turns me on to watch you pleasure yourself."

"Why would something like that get you hot?" She sighed as he pinched the rosy buds between his fingers.

"Are you not beautiful? Why wouldn't the sight of you excite a man? I'm not in any hurry to end the night, are you?"

She shuddered. "No."

He knelt in front of her, and gazed over her body. She squirmed beneath his hands as he learned her curves. "You're perfect. Hasn't anyone told you that before?" He continued to explore her, touching every part of her splendid skin.

She parted her lips as if to to speak, yet only a long, heavy breath released. "Your skin is so flawless_you have no idea how much I want you."

"Tell me?"

He grinned. How she teased him. "Every time I touch you, my cock throbs. When I see your eyes burn with desire, it drives my mind to places I cannot control."

She widened her thighs in an offering, and the warmth of her pussy called to him. He yearned to feel her damp skin, but restrained himself, not wanting to hurry the moment. Once he made contact with her sensitive flesh, he doubted he'd stop.

He placed kisses on her thighs making his way back up toward her stomach. At her belly button, he dipped his tongue in and her breath left her lungs in a loud gasp. He gripped her sweet ass, massaging her cheeks, marveling in her perfection.

"This Gerrid who let you go was an utter idiot." He continued to caress her bottom in his firm grip. It pleased him that she hadn't denied his compliment. So turned on, she accepted his praises without a fight. After a final squeeze, he stood and threaded his fingers through hers. Her lips parted in clear invitation and he angled his mouth across hers for a sweet embrace.

The tantalizing flowery smell of her, the feel of her, consumed him. How could any man refuse such a woman? He'd never deny her, always keep her happy...but dreaming of the impossible wouldn't get him anywhere. He trailed his mouth along her jaw, down to the base of her neck.

"You're an incredible kisser," she practically purred.

He smiled against her skin. Years of practice had gifted him. He pressed his tongue against her pulse point and she tensed. Startled by her unexpected reaction, he jerked his head up to find her wide-eyed.

"You're too good to be true," she said.

He tsked. "You're already resorting to your old self. Let go of your thoughts." He arched an eyebrow. "Wasn't that the purpose of our encounter?"

"I just...."

"You're waiting for the bomb to drop?"

She nodded. "Yes, that's exactly right."

"Has anything happened to you so far to warrant such feelings?" He slid his touch along her jaw.

"No."

"So your concerns are without merit. This isn't only for you, but for me also." He owed her the truth. She hadn't spoken a word he didn't believe was complete honesty; she'd earned the same respect.

"What do you get out of this?"

He grinned. "I get to prove you wrong."

"Wrong about what?"

He pushed every ounce of his emotions to the surface of his expression. "That you're not a lost woman."

Her brows furrowed and the arousal raging in her gaze faded. Something he'd rectify. He kissed his way down to her chest and teased her taut buds. He cupped both breasts together and licked one a nipple at a time. "Tell me where and how to touch you?"

She worried her bottom lip. Here stood the woman he sought to rid her of—shy, broken, and tentative. He'd seen flashes of the commanding soul inside her. But numerous times so far, insecurity would stop her, and she'd become embarrassed at being so forthright.

"I ask again—what would you like me to do?"

Instead of using her voice, she ran her hand over her stomach until she cupped her mound.

"Ah, I see. But tell me with words."

"I can't," she whispered.

He folded his arms over his chest in a show of defiance. "It's a real pity I have to leave you standing there craving me until you're able."

Indecision flared in her eyes. Finally, after long moments, she cleared her throat. "Fine. Play with my pussy."

How he lusted to feel her; to spread her juices along his fingers, but her curt tone told him he needed to push harder. "Instruct me exactly how you want it."

Her eyes went huge and her cheeks flushed. "Like step-by-step detail?"

"You did say you want to be the woman you used to be. The naïve one who believed everything and anything could be possible. A lady such as that would have no fear because there would be no repercussions."

Determination rose in her expression. "Run your fingers along the sides of my pussy, gently."

He did as she asked and her head fell back. "Is this what you're after?"

"Yes. Tickle me."

The pounding of her heart filled his ears, calling for his fangs to sink into her neck, yet he ignored the impulse. "What is it you ask of me now?"

"Feel the wetness."

He eased his touch over her swollen flesh until he met the moisture there. He dragged the silkiness over her sensitive skin, earning him a full body shudder from her.

"Oh, my God." Her legs wobbled. "Circle my clit."

He pressed against her swollen nub and her knees gave out. He wrapped an arm around her waist to offer support. Her sexy sigh sounded next to his ear, causing him to grunt. Sure if he didn't hurry her along with his plan it would fall to pieces, he shifted her until she was stable on her feet, then moved away from her. He wanted her on the rock for a reason. Her confidence had been shattered, and he knew even if he told her she was special, she'd never believe him.

Cupping her head, he stared into her hooded eyes. "I ask again, do you trust me?"

She nodded.

"Then, please, do as I ask and get up on the rock."

CHAPTER THREE

Ellie's mind raced. Somehow she doubted he wanted her up on the boulder to just sit there. Could she follow through with whatever he asked?

Only one way to find out!

The dirty talk alone made her ready to beg for more, but his touch set her aflame. She slid across the flat surface and watched Bryce resume his spot in the chair.

Leaning back, he rested his elbows on the armrests. His voice dropped an octave. "Spread your thighs."

She thought it strange that she listened to him without pause. Her old self would never have considered exposing herself in such a manner, but she'd never see him again. The knowledge allowed her a sense of freedom; the ability to act without any fear of repercussions. She spread herself wide for him.

"Lovely." He leaned forward in his chair. "Show me how to pleasure you right."

"What is it you are asking me to do, exactly?"

He grinned, the sexiest damn thing she'd ever seen. "I did tell you I'd learn about you from the way you moan, did I not?"

Understanding drifted up. "Are you asking me to play with myself?"

"No." He arched an eyebrow. "I want to watch you come."

She'd masturbated many times, but alone. Having his gorgeous eyes on her while she brought herself to orgasm wasn't a horrible thought. But doubt tightened her stomach. "What if I can't?"

"Do you need me to help you along?"

"I do."

The corner of his mouth arched up. "Stroke your pussy. Is it wet?"

She slid along the trimmed hair until she met silky dampness. "Yes."

"Perfect. Drag your splendid juices to your clit."

Her skin grew slick with her arousal and she circled her nub. Wild sensations stole her breath. "Mmm...." The sensations demanded she close her eyes, but she couldn't pull herself away from him.

Part of her knew better than to believe what happened with Gerrid could be her fault. But a little voice always reminded her if she'd been more, been better, he wouldn't have looked elsewhere. Bryce caressed the broken part of her soul and awakened an unknown strength inside her.

She rolled her clit and shivered, the pleasure sending her thoughts from her mind. More. Pressing harder, she panted, overwhelmed by glorious sensations.

Dipping inside the moisture, she teased her soft flesh as shudders erupted through her. Her head fell back and she circled her hips in the rhythm she set.

So close.

Almost there.

Desperately seeking more fuel to find her release, she snapped her head back to him. Her pussy convulsed as she stared into the face of a pure, hungry man.

She imagined his mouth on her, licking at her breasts, running his tongue along her dampened skin. The sensations intensified. She angled her hips and pushed harder against herself to climax. Light danced before her vision. Nothing else existed, no broken heart, no thoughts of hard times, only a complete, succulent explosion.

A warm, wet embrace forced her back to awareness. Bryce knelt between her thighs, naked. *How did he have the time to remove his clothes?* She might have considered it more, if the feeling of him along her moist heat didn't take precedent.

He lapped up the evidence of her release. "So sweet. So delicious." He grunted, dipping inside her and went wild with his tongue.

His skill sent her sky bound. She squirmed and cried out under the efforts of his marvelous mouth.

He was everywhere and she reeled in the superb sensations. He brought her clit out from its hood and her eyes rolled back into her head. He sucked deep and she thrust herself against him.

Tingles erupted from the top of her head, right down to her toes then the world as she knew it ceased to exist. Her pussy contracted as she came against his mouth. After a sweet kiss on her thigh, he backed away and stood up. He tickled her bottom lip with his finger. She opened her mouth and allowed him in. His skin dragged against her tongue and she pulled in her cheeks around him.

He grinned, dropping his fingers down to tease her entrance. Heat pooled in her center. He pushed inside of her and the stretch he provided was thick enough causing her to sigh.

"You're so tight." His voice sounded deep, rich with lust, and the sound shivered down her spine.

"I haven't been with anyone in a while...." She gasped as he hit a sweet spot. Her eyes watered. She tensed when he surged upward. "Oh, that's good."

He worked the area with continuous flicks. She shouted out her pleasure, not caring who heard. He placed his free hand over her womb and without a hint of warning, he thrust his fingers deeper into her, full of purpose.

Stars twinkled before her vision.

She gritted her teeth as the sensation built and her sounds of satisfaction soared across the night sky. He remained focused on her, yet he blurred as he pushed in and out. Every nerve ending in her body rejoiced as she lost herself completely and wetness warmed her thighs.

When the world returned to her, she giggled, attempting to recover from the ride he'd sent her on. Her bottom numb from resting on such a hard surface. "How did you do that?" He'd made her come in a way she never had before, and the aftershocks still lingered within her.

"You've never been treated right." His stern tone matched the seriousness in his expression. "That's going to change."

Did he promise her more orgasms? Part of her hoped he did. The other part wondered if she'd survive.

With the haze of her climax fading, she admired him. Long, lean muscles, defined ridges of abs calling her to trace each curve to the splendid V on his hips, and further, leading to his fabulous, thick cock.

Her hand twitched to reach out to him. To offer the same pleasure he'd given her. She leaned toward him, but he latched onto her wrist and shook his head. "It's not about me_only you."

He whisked her off the rock and carried her through the back door of the house.

Plain white walls, rich color accents, abstract paintings that not only were beautiful, but appeared expensive, decorated the interior of the home. Ellie inhaled the rich scent of spice that seemed to belong to Bryce, mixed with the warm vanilla scents carried in the home. He strode up the stairs heading straight toward a room at the end of the hall.

He entered, and she discovered a large, clean, space, bare except for a king size bed mounted on a dark wooden platform against the back wall.

"Come here, let me feel you." He placed her on the mattress, grabbed her thighs, and pulled her toward him.

The man above her was made of heaven. She might have doubted his perfection, attempted to piece together his game to determine how he played her, but she couldn't be bothered to care. She wanted to be played, good and hard.

He leaned down and pressed his lips on hers, offering slow and savoring kisses.

She melted into him and missed his touch when he drew away. He reached into the bedside table and grabbed a condom. "I'm assuming you would like me to use protection?"

"You're right." One-night stands were fun, but getting an STD didn't appeal to her. She snatched up the condom. "Let me."

He leaned back. "By all means."

After she unwrapped the condom, she grabbed his cock and stroked it. He tensed, causing his glorious muscles to bulge. "Best get that on. If you keep jerking me off, this isn't going to last long."

She rolled the latex down to the base of his shaft. He gathered her in his arms, flipping positions so he lay on his back and she straddled him.

"Have your way with me." He winked.

She placed her hands on his chest and rose up then squirmed onto him. Her inner walls strained against his girth. Slow and steady, she accepted him, waiting for her muscles to loosen to settle him in deep.

Caressing her breasts, she moved up and down on his shaft. The burn in his gaze deepened and nearly made her increase her speed, but she restrained herself, desperate to draw the moment out.

She raised herself to the tip of his cock and bounced, only to slowly devour him again. His throaty groan formed goose bumps along her skin and she echoed the sound. She explored his chest, the curves of his abs, and his muscles flexed beneath her hands.

"You're a sexy woman, Ellie. I love how you fondle yourself to entice me and then how you touch me as if nothing has ever felt so good." He pushed on her chest, forcing her back. Her hands caught her weight and she placed them on his thighs behind her. She pumped herself along his shaft.

"That feels amazing." She'd never been so brazen. Never showed so much of herself while she worked a cock, but how could she deny him?

"Tell me." His voice sounded strangled. "Are you ready?"

She rode him nice and slow to tease him. "For what?"

"To come." He lifted her above him and gave a hard thrust.

She gasped out in surprise.

"Your climax is right there, isn't it?" He didn't wait for her response. Instead, he unleashed himself and fucked her senseless.

Her only recourse was to squeal. The sensation she'd felt when he fingered her rose again, but this time it became even stronger. The sounds escaping her mouth liquefied into an all-encompassing shout of pleasure.

"Don't stop fucking me." Her pussy clamped down and tingles erupted throughout her body.

He dug his fingers into her bottom. "I don't intend to."

She teetered on the edge of her release. But as he pounded into her with a strength no man should possess, the wave broke and she soared into orgasm.

Slamming down onto him, the space between their bodies felt wet, warm, and sticky. She fell forward and dropped her head on his chest in an attempt to catch her breath. After some time, she managed to move. "If you keep giving making me come like that, I'm not sure I'll survive the night."

"You'll enjoy every release I give to you." He kissed her lips, shifted out from under her, and jumped up. He strode into the adjoining bathroom, while she settled back on the bed.

She'd never come so much...well, ever!

He returned carrying a small container. She raised her head to examine the contents. "What's that for?"

"You shall see." He spread the shiny liquid along his fingers before closing the lid and placing the container on the end table.

He's not going to...?

Oh yes, the implication was quite clear. Where else would he put a finger loaded with lube? She gulped.

"You have the control here. Whenever you don't like something, tell me and I will stop." He shifted her onto her side, pulling her knee up to her chest and settled in behind her. "But you, Ellie, I think will love this."

She squeaked when he placed his cock at her entrance again and pushed through. He dipped his hand between her ass cheeks and rubbed her anus. She tensed. "There's nothing to fear." His rough breath sounded next to her ear. "Has no one ever touched you here before?" He circled the bud, spreading the silkiness along her skin.

"No," she managed.

He inserted a finger inside her tight knot. With his cock working inside of her and his finger stretching her ass, nothing had ever felt so good. "Do you like this?"

"Yes." She exhaled.

He steadied his digit, holding it still while his cock worked in her slick heat. "I'd be honored if you would grant me the right to give you every orgasm possible. Will you trust that I won't hurt you?"

"I do."

He withdrew from her body and she glanced over her shoulder to see him removing the condom and applying a new one. He spread the lubrication over the latex and along her skin. The silkiness felt sexy and kinky.

He raised her thigh higher and his cock pushed against her anus as he circled her clit. Her heart raced and her muscles tightened. He lowered his lips down to her neck. His hot breath against her nape was more than enough to send her worries astray, but the hard pressure against her nub sent flashes of pleasure to vanish her apprehensions completely.

"Relax." His gentleness made time slow. Her impatience rose. She pushed back against him and the tip of his cock dipped through the rim. The tightness elevated, replaced by a sensation she hadn't expected—she was so perfectly full. Each rub against her bundle of nerves sent a rush of tingles that traveled down to her stretched ass.

Once he seated himself fully, he stilled. "Are you in pain?"

"No."

His voice dipped lower. "Do you want me to stop?"

"No."

"Good, because nothing pleases me more than to be right

here." He played with her clit, moving his cock in and out of her. The sensation was by far the strangest she'd ever experienced. Intense and mind blowing. He increased his speed and she grasped the bed sheets. His thrusts came hard against her bottom. He lowered his mouth to her shoulder and his teeth penetrated her skin.

She screamed at the invasion. He'd been so gentle. Biting her with such strength wasn't called for. Yet, the moment he sucked against her skin, thought ceased to exist. She buried her face against the pillow and erupted into a woman satisfied to the bone. He pushed deep into her ass, while his body shook with his own release.

Sweat beaded her forehead, and she tried to regain her strength. But when he licked her shoulder, her mind rebounded, and she jerked her head toward him. "You like to bite, do you?"

He chuckled. "Just a little nibble."

She ran her hand over her skin, expecting to find evidence of his hard bite, but her fingers came back dry. She could've sworn blood had dripped down her back. He slid out of the bed and headed for the bathroom, only to return a moment later with a dampened washcloth.

"Here, let me wash you." He cleaned her, then himself, before he returned the cloth to the bathroom. Joining her again, he gathered her in his arms, spooning her. He trailed his fingers along the curve of her hipbone and gave the spot where he bit her a kiss. "You're tired, rest."

Here, in the warmth of his embrace, sleep sounded like a great idea.

Chapter Four

Bryce's immortal life wasn't one he'd force on another—lonely nights and dead days were his to suffer alone. His glanced over her beautiful face, to her perky breasts, along the lines of her womanly figure to the fleshy part of her thighs. Breathtaking. Maybe some men would miss the subtleness that made her glow, but she enamored him. She'd proven to be far more trusting than he'd expected or thought he deserved.

On many occasions, he'd set up the same scene, desperate to see a woman bring herself to the highest level of arousal by her own hand. No one ever complied. Some too shy, others not comfortable with the idea of masturbating in front of him. He hadn't expected Ellie to be so valiant. Her boldness, though, didn't stem from an inborn trait, but devised of a plan to prove something to herself. Yet, she'd gathered the courage to get past her fears and act because he asked it of her.

Her faith touched him. If only he could stay longer with her, but how could he? His existence was a myth—a story told to scare children. She'd never understand even if she did believe him. Prolonging the inevitable would be pointless. No, he would leave her.

He trailed his finger along her spine and she stirred, lifting her head. "How long did I sleep?"

"Not long, only an hour or so." He continued the path he drew on her back and the blood that flowed beneath her skin called to him. How delicious she'd tasted when he fed from her. Sweet and innocent. It titillated his senses. "Sunrise comes in an hour or so. I'm going to have to leave you soon."

She glanced around the room before focusing back on him. "How do you know what time it is? There's no clock here?"

He shrugged. "It's a talent."

"One that tells you when the sun rises?"

"You got it." He smacked her ass and her luscious, sweet chuckle made his cock awaken. "If I may, can I have one last indulgence in your body?"

She snuggled into him. "I want the very same thing, but there's something I'd love to do first." She got up onto her knees, pushed against him to hold him in place. He grinned, allowing her to think she could overpower him. He found her so lovely. She'd woven a spell over him in such a short time.

Her soft breasts skimmed over him as she went lower. How he'd enjoy placing his cock in her cleavage and fucking her tits. However, she stayed on her journey, and he did not intend to stop her.

He sensed her breath along his erection before she wrapped a hand around his shaft. "I've wanted to do take you into my mouth all night," she purred.

The purely feminine sound hardened his cock to near impossible limits. "Then take what you are after."

The head of his dick touched her soft, plush lips right before she drew him in. Moist and warm. He found his utopia. She drew in her cheeks around him, bringing him deep into her throat.

She worked his shaft with a determination that could easily make him come. He wanted to stay this way, reveling in her sweetness, but he yearned to feel her moist heat once more. Her gaze stayed focused on his eyes while she sucked him, relentless. The trepidatious woman he first met didn't remain in her any longer. He brushed his fingers across her cheek. "Your mouth is heaven."

She teased the slit with her tongue. "I'm enjoying this too." She licked down the base of his shaft until she came to his sack, where she sucked his testicles. Then, she cupped him and licked behind.

The moment she connected with the taint, he bucked upward. "Keep going."

She kept at him with deliberate flicks. Sounds of satisfaction poured from his mouth, and he realized if he didn't get away from her, he wouldn't last a minute longer. "Fuck," he roared. His balls tightened and his stomach tensed with the sign of his release.

He reached over to grab another condom and applied it with haste. He hoped to see her healed, to give her something to always remember him by, but he planned to fuck her in the way his cock demanded. He grabbed her by the waist and brought her up to her knees. He didn't even bother to check if her pussy was slick; his cock touched her gentle folds and he entered her with one steady push.

Her gasp echoed off the walls, not only tender, but he suspected that by her sharp inhale she hungered for him with an equal force. He grabbed onto her hips, eyed her heart shaped ass, and waited a mere moment before he thrust against her in an act to satisfy himself. Her back arched and, fuck, did it bring him in deep.

"Do you like being taken from behind?"

"Yes." She exhaled. "Don't be gentle. Give it to me hard."

He slapped her rump with a flat handed hit, before he spread her cheeks, allowing him to fill her deeper. He pounded against her, not to punish her, but to intensify her pleasure.

"Oh God, yes...."

He snatched her up and shifted to the side of the mattress. She squealed when he slid her off the bed. "What are you doing?" She gripped his forearms tight.

"Trust me." He kept a firm hold on her, lowering her head to the ground. With her shoulders resting against the wood floor, he lifted her hips, settling her in the right position. He straddled her ass, while he put his hands on her thighs to push them down so her feet settled by her head.

"Well, this is certainly different." She chortled. He slid into her hot, wet pussy. Her laughter died off and her pupils dilated. "But good...."

He held his erection and angled it down while he used the other hand to work her clit.

"Oh my God...oh....."

Her flexibility added to the position; her feet remained by her head, which only opened her more for him. So deep. She accepted every inch of him, right to his balls. Her face flushed and her pussy pulsated around him. It drove him wild. He increased his speed, her eyes widened, and her expression swept away with pleasure. The sounds from her mouth hitched, and soon after, her breath froze. He deepened his cock thrusts, slammed harder against her, forcing her to release.

Her inner walls clamped against him so tight. He stilled, waiting for the tension to cease, not wanting to blow inside of her since he didn't want this to end.

The furrow of her brows and the tautness of her mouth softened. She blinked. "Give me more."

"Gladly." He pulled her up off the floor, placing her stomach down on the bed, and yanked her hips back so they were off the edge. Grasping her hips, he raised her up, seated himself at her entrance and thrust in.

"Je-su-s..." sounded from her mouth through the steady streams of unforgiving thrusts.

She relaxed around him and allowed him to hold her weight. It made the man inside him roar. Her trust astounded him. He'd given her a night of pleasure, and she returned the favor, allowing him to have his way with her.

He craved more. Wrapping his arms around her waist, he picked her up so her back lay against his chest. "I promise to not let you fall." He turned, her legs wrapped around him tight, and he lowered her face-first toward the floor. She squealed, reaching out to brace herself.

He shifted his feet out shoulder width apart in order to stabilize himself, and without pause he gave it to her.

Hard.

Rough.

Her shouts of ecstasy poured around him as he pummeled into her. The pit of his stomach tightened, his cock burned to release, but his fangs pressed again his gums, demanding blood.

Fighting against himself, he withdrew, and she cried out. "Get back in there and finish me."

He smiled, settling her back to the ground. The redness of her face drained removing the blood that rushed there.

She frowned at him. "Did you come?"

"Not likely, luv." He arched his eyebrow. "Ready for more?"

"Damn right I am." She raised herself off the floor, stepped in close to him and her taut nipples pressed on his chest. He gathered her legs to wrap around his waist and sat on the bed. She lowered down onto him, then rocked her hips. Pleasure made him blind, his dick smacked against her inner walls, and her eyes widened.

The more she shifted, the more confidence she gained, and in no time she fucked him without mercy. Her sweaty skin gleamed against the light, lust written hard on her face, and her mouth parted as she sought air.

He'd been careful to take from her shoulder before. Now, selfishness surrounded him. He yearned to bite into her large vein and draw thick blood on his tongue. He grasped her hair and yanked her head to the side. The throes of her release brought the perfect time to act. He opened his mouth, exposed his fangs, and sank his teeth into her sweet, warm skin.

Sensory overload struck him as her hot blood poured into his mouth and emptied down his throat. She trembled around him while her arousal dampened his lap. He drew long and deep against the puncture marks. He'd savor her and wouldn't waste a drop of her sweetness.

He continued drinking her up until she quieted. Making quick work of healing the wounds, he lapped up any escaping blood.

She stayed silent, recovering, until finally she looked at him. "You, Bryce, can bite me any damn time you want."

Fear made him speechless. *Does she know?*

CHAPTER FIVE

Ellie could only be glad she didn't have to move; her muscles held no strength. Lying on her side, she faced Bryce. The mysterious nature of this man captivated her.

"I need to say something before I leave you," he said.

"What do you mean leave? Aren't you going to drive me home?" Sure, she didn't expect an invitation to stay over into the next day, but a gentleman would ensure she returned to her house. From what she'd seen of him so far, he didn't seem the type to forget his manners.

He brushed his finger across her cheek. "I'm sorry, but we spent too much time together and I have somewhere to go before the sun rises. Rest awhile then call a taxi to take you home."

His longing expression told another story. She raised her head off the pillow. "What's wrong?"

"Let go," he whispered.

She laughed. "I'm pretty sure I just did that, repeatedly."

"No." His voice sounded sharp and commanding. "Release the pain in your heart. Don't let one experience forever change you. You're too special to allow one person to alter your life."

His words struck a chord and her hurt emotions rose. "How do I forget?"

"You don't let the dream fade away." He placed his hand over her heart. "What lies in here is something wonderful, something that could make a man happy, but if you don't remember the woman you are, it'll be lost forever. You'll end up living a life you don't deserve."

She shook her head, determined to prove him wrong. "It's not there anymore." Nothing could bring her old self back. Gerrid had ruined the dreams she once held.

"It's there—you only have to see it," he countered. "Did you not feel your heart touching mine?"

"But what does it matter? We both know this night was about one thing only. The exact thing we both asked Madame Eve to find us—a one-night stand."

"Do we?" He arched an eyebrow. "Fate brought you and I together to experience each other and to gain something from that adventure. What I'll take with me is the joy of seeing a woman who was a little lost, but opened herself to new possibilities again."

"If what you say is true, why are you saying goodbye? If you saw something in me you think is so special, why don't you stay?"

His eyes lowered and raw pain swept his expression. "Because I'm not the one destined to love you."

"Why should I believe you then?"

He cupped her face. "If I could remain here with you, I would. But I am....I'm not meant to share a life with you. We only have this night, and I'll never forget our time together. You've made me feel alive. There's so much darkness in our world, but within it, there are beams of light, such as yourself, who bring a reminder to me that life is special." His grip tightened around her cheeks. "Always share yourself. Don't hide behind unhappy memories because it'd be a damn shame for you not to remember who you are."

She sighed. "I'm not sure I know who I am anymore. Even with Gerrid, I'd become someone different, conforming to be the woman he desired. I've been lost for so long."

"Sure you do. You showed me her. She's a woman who lives without boundaries, who trusted when she had no reason to, who believes in chance and thinks that anything is possible. Someone who tries new things because she wants more from her life, even if she hesitates, because in the end she is searching for her happily ever after."

"So, that's what the night was all about? What you were to me?" Looking back, she could see how every moment, everything he said to her, led to her discovering herself again.

He smiled. "I was exactly what you needed. Fate brought you a reminder, and you'll choose how you take it and go from here."

Fate—more like Madame Eve.

He settled in behind her and brushed his lips on her shoulder. "Promise you'll always remember me, and most of all, you'll never forget yourself."

"I'll try to."

He seemed too good to be true. Too experienced. Too perfect. Had her fantasy come true and given her the man she always dreamed of? His presence seemed dreamlike. His ability to move so fast, undress in a blink of an eye, suggested something more existed in him, but what?

"I'll never forget you," he whispered, a sound filled with such longing it clenched her heart.

A gust of wind came from behind her, raising goose bumps along her skin. She startled, sitting up. "Bryce?"

One second here, the next gone.

Right then, her phone rang, jolting her off the bed. Her purse rested by the door, but when had Bryce gotten it from the car?

Ignoring the mess of her mind, she dropped to her knees and grabbed her phone. "Hello."

"Well hell, there you are, sex kitten." Kenna's amused tone sounded through the speaker. "Tell me everything and don't leave a single, juicy detail out."

"I don't think you'd believe me even if I told you."

A moment of silence hit the other end of the phone, before Kenna piped up, "That good of a night, was it?"

She thought back over her time with Bryce, her mind spinning to figure out how he left so fast. Did she dream him? No, she couldn't be dreaming if she were still in his house. But one thing she did know was the woman who stepped into this house wasn't the one who knelt on the hardwood floor. "More than good—the most incredible night of my life. Listen, I'll tell you everything later, but if you wouldn't mind, would you come and get me."

"What! You're still at his house? He didn't bring you home?"

How to put this? He up and vanished? She doubted Kenna would believe her and she really didn't want to be laughed at. "No, he just left."

"What do you mean, he just left?" Protective best friend to the rescue.

"He...er...got called away."

"So, he left you in his house, alone?"

"Um, yeah."

"What an asshole," Kenna spat. "Where are you? I'll come and get you."

"Well...." She got to her feet, spotting some mail on the nightstand. She snatched it up and read off the address.

"Got it," Kenna replied. "I'll be there in twenty."

She sighed. "Thanks."

"No problem, babe. I can't believe he left you there." She hesitated. "Hey, Ellie, are you okay?"

The thought of never seeing Bryce again hurt. He'd touched her heart. Reminded her of something she simply couldn't see before. The bad happenings didn't shape her life; moments like these were what defined her.

Gerrid introduced her to love. Bryce confirmed it existed and showed her there could be more out there for her.

She tried to focus on how much he'd changed her life in the few hours they'd been together. At least, she fooled herself into believing she'd concentrate on the good. She spoke from her heart. "I haven't quite decided yet."

$$\mathcal{L}$$

Bryce had fled to the basement. A room he'd built to protect him from the Miami sun. No windows, steel door locked from the inside—the safest place for him to be at sunrise. He listened to Ellie's phone conversation. A smile rose to his face as he heard the tiredness from their escapade in her voice, and it pleased him to recount the night himself.

Warmth touched his cold soul. Women came into his life and left just as fast. He'd always felt good about what he'd done for them, given them a night with a man who cared and marveled over them, but no one made*him*feel happy. What would it be like to share his life with Ellie?

He shook his head, trying to remove the thought from his mind. Vampires couldn't find love with mortals. He'd resolved years ago to do what he did for Ellie, help women who needed to be reminded of their worth.

Besides, how would she react if she found out his true nature? Run in fear, he suspected, just as the love of his life did before her. Spending time dreaming would get him nowhere. Her life would be better than if he'd not met her and he fed.

Why, though, did he not feel satisfied? The more he lay on his plush bed, wrapped in silk sheets, the more he tried to battle against his desire to keep her.

He heard her end the call and begin dressing. His throat tightened. If his heart still beat, he assumed it'd be thumping hard. Thoughts rushed in his mind, going back and forth and fighting against each other.

Her footsteps sounded above him as she hurried down the stairs. Each one pulled at him. In seconds, she'd be gone, forever.

No.

His heart told him, *Stop her.*

He threw off the sheets, still naked, and rushed toward the door. He'd never been so unsure of himself, and he couldn't quite explain why he acted now, only knowing he held no other choice.

The lock clicked open and he bolted from the basement as the sunlight peered through the windows. "Ellie," he called out.

At the front door, she turned and horror flashed in her eyes. He glanced down to his arms, seeing them smolder from the sun. Without pause, he stepped back into shadows of the basement doorway. She ran toward him at full, mortal speed.

"Oh, God, you're on fire."

"No, it's fine." He pulled her down the stairs and into his room. Closing the door, he turned back to her. "Give me your arm."

Her eyes shone with confusion, yet she reached out and he grabbed her wrist, bringing it to his mouth. He released his fangs, witnessing her pale with fear before he sank his teeth into her skin, hearing her gasp.

She trembled and stared at the burn marks as they healed. "What are you?" she whispered.

He sealed up the puncture marks with his tongue, preparing for her to leave. "Vampire."

She examined her skin, then looked over his forearms. He wished he could see into her mind and cursed his inability to read her thoughts. "The wounds, the bite marks you gave me, they're gone." She glanced at him with wide, surprised eyes. "Vampires are real?"

"Indeed they are."

She drew in a shaky breath. "If someone told me this I never would've believed it. But the things I saw tonight—I knew you were different." She eyed him, curiously. "How long have you been this way?"

He couldn't believe she still stood here in front of him, but rejoiced that she did. "For many years."

She blinked. "How did this happen to you?"

"Times were different back then. Vampires were vicious and destroyed lives without thought. Another of my kind saved me, a man of generous heart, and without him, I doubt I'd still be here."

"Do other people know vampires are real?"

He shrugged. "Some do, but not many."

She studied him. "Why are you telling me this?"

"Because I don't want you to go."

Her eyes rimmed with tears. A wave of shock tensed his muscles. A woman showing emotion toward *him*. How long had it been? Too long. His dead heart swelled.

Without a word to him, she dug into her purse, pulled out her phone, and typed a number. Two rings sounded before a woman answered. "Kenna, it's me. Don't come and get me." She paused. "Yes, I'm fine. Bryce is back, and I'm going to stay with him." She ended the call.

He greatly admired her. She'd heard his secret and faced it, dead on. No matter that he could hear her racing heartbeat, she didn't run away. "Do you understand what this will mean for you?"

"No," she answered. "But I'm interested in finding out."

"You have no idea how happy I am to hear that, but...." She deserved the truth before she got in over her head. "I have a shadowed soul, Ellie."

Stepping forward, she pressed her body against his and smiled. "Your soul is no more shadowed than my own."

He never expected to find something so special in her when Madame Eve arranged their pairing. Ellie made him feel alive by the way she trusted him, and he saw the possibility of a future. He'd told her of his dark life, and there she stood, staring up at him as if she'd saved him—not the other way around.

"Where do we go from here?" she whispered.

"We get to know each other better, fall in love, and when you're ready...." He pressed his lips against hers, wrapping his arms around her so tight. "I'll give you forever."

FOREVER BOUND

BY

STACEY KENNEDY

CHAPTER ONE

J osie Harper's nerves were rattled. She'd never expected to have to hire someone to see her fantasies met. Sometimes, though, life doesn't turn out how one expects it.

There had been plenty of boyfriends, lovers, and even friends with benefits in her life. None, though, could satisfy her. Not only in life, but sexually. Something had always been missing, something she needed to find. Those were the reasons she flew from Dallas to Las Vegas and why she stood in the elevator at the Castillo Resort and Hotel. The night may drain her savings account, one she'd added to over the twenty-five years of her life, but it didn't matter. Not anymore. Sick of feeling unhappy, tired of not experiencing fulfillment, she'd been left with no other choice.

The question needed to be answered, *Is BDSM meant for me?*

She'd looked into her options for her self-discovery experiment, and had come across all sorts of avenues. Should she join a club with others who lived the BDSM lifestyle? She'd run across personal ads in the local newspaper and even classes offering to teach novices. But Madame Eve's 1NightStand solution offered the most privacy.

Josie's interests...well, she hadn't quite figured them out yet. The idea of being dominated appealed to her. Images of being bound to a table while being spanked created heat between her thighs. But were these just fantasies or did she want to *live* the lifestyle?

Josie'd spent a good part of a day filling out a questionnaire given to her by 1NightStand detailing what she wanted, and even needed, from the experience. Had informed the woman of things she'd do and not do so the Dom would understand her limits.

Days after she'd faxed the questionnaire back, Josie received an email from Madame Eve confirming she'd made a match for her. The illusive Madame Eve found her a man to lead her into undiscovered territory?

It appeared she had. Was she ready to do this now? Push all her reservations aside and have the naughty sex which only lived in her dreams? Doubt nagged her. What else could be expected? The situation was new to her and not what anyone would call *normal*. She'd come for a reason though. She couldn't let unease make her act stupidly.

She pushed away the fear and straightened her shoulders. The email stated for her to go to the fourth floor, room *412*. They'd have complete privacy since the floor would be free of guests, and the room soundproofed, but a telephone would be available in case she became uneasy and needed a safety net.

As the elevator came to a stop, she stood for so long she wondered if she'd lost her nerve. *None of that.* Stepping through the open doors, she blew out a long, deep breath to gather herself.

Each step felt like a lifetime. What type of man would Gavin be? Handsome? Powerful? Butterflies whipped through her stomach at the images playing in her mind.

Reaching the last door on the right, she stopped and drew in a sharp breath. She'd come for a reason and no matter how much hesitation she felt, she forced herself to open the door.

The scene before her was not at all what she'd expected to find. Yes, she wanted ropes, but this hadn't been what she meant—two waist-high steel poles with a rope strung between them, stretched from one side of the bare room to the other. She wondered what would take place there, with its walls painted a crimson red and candles scattered throughout on black satin covered tables.

The only other items in the room, a large rope resting on the hardwood floor, along with a smaller one, and one hanging from the ceiling with a loop clamp on it. As much as she tried to come up with a reason for all this, her thoughts just couldn't wrap around it. She'd thought of flogging, leather, chains, bondage. Never just ropes in a stark room. For the life of her, she didn't understand what she faced. Just as her mind threatened to run away with her, the door handle jiggled behind her, and she turned as it opened. A man, smooth and confident, entered the room.

Madame Eve had picked her perfect match indeed, everything her dreams were made of and more. Tanned and shirtless, with hard lines of muscles, dressed in a pair of dark jeans, he looked delicious. His outfit not at all what she'd expected, leather pants would have been more appropriate. Not saying his attire displeased her—he looked spectacular.

Dark hair covered his forehead in a wispy way, and deep chocolate eyes spoke of the pleasure awaiting her. Her heart thumped in her chest. The hesitation she experienced earlier, fled. His poise, the subtle way he held himself, comforted her.

Tonight, he'd be her Dom and she craved to submit.

Gavin longed for the perfect submissive. A woman worthy of the gift he could give her. He went to the clubs in the Las Vegas area, assisted other Doms in learning how to handle their subs, but it hadn't gotten him anywhere close to finding his own fulfillment. When he'd heard of Madame Eve's 1NightStand, he'd jumped on it. He didn't believe she would find him his happily ever after. Curiosity made him act.

It'd been two years since he'd last had a submissive and he couldn't see that changing any time soon. Not to say the women he'd met hadn't been exquisite in their own right. The connection, the roar to own someone else but have them captivating enough for him to hold their wants over his own, didn't exist. In truth, he hadn't met anyone deserving of it. Most failed to meet his expectations. He'd been a demanding Dom and had yet to meet a woman he could push as far as he wanted.

It left him unsatisfied.

Madame Eve emailed to say she had a perfect match for him and gave him enough insight on Josie to give him an idea of how he should set up the scene. He wondered if Madame Eve had indeed filled her obligation, if Josie might be a perfect match for him, though he doubted it. Nevertheless, he indulged in the experience.

Standing before Josie, shock made him stop. In all his time as a Dom to new people who wanted to learn about the lifestyle, none of them looked like her.

Long, dirty blonde hair surrounded a gorgeous face. Her blue eyes, wide with innocence, stared at him. He questioned if he'd entered the right room. The woman looked like a girl next door, not the typical type he encountered. With flushed cheeks as though embarrassed, her pouty mouth held a nervous smile.

Truth was Madame Eve had given him an extensive knowledge of Josie's limits. Hearing the woman wanted to be bound by ropes hadn't surprised him, yet seeing Josie, timid and trembling, did. He arched an eyebrow. "Josie?"

She nodded shyly. "You're Gavin, right?"

Excitement coursed through him at her acknowledgment. To most, it'd be her perfect-ten figure to bring forth arousal. Not for Gavin. For him, the sweet note about her, her gentleness showing the need to please is what held his interest. It wouldn't have shocked him to hear she was a straight *A* student in college and lived by the book in every regard. Always said the right thing, did the right thing, and behaved as the general public would want her to.

However, he witnessed the barrier she held up. The front she erected around herself to always please the ones around her. To be what others thought she should be. All of these things enthralled him. She wanted to please, but also wanted to release the untamed beast inside her.

Honor touched his soul to be granted the right to assist her. Locking the door behind him, he dropped the bag slung over his shoulder and approached her. As he drew closer, her breathing deepened and the blush on her cheeks grew.

He'd set up the scene earlier that evening, keeping in mind she'd never experienced BSDM before. The scene before them would introduce her to the lifestyle on her own terms. Yes, he would have a part in the experience, but he would seek no pleasure for himself.

Not to say he wouldn't find it pleasurable. Watching Josie would give him the satisfaction he longed for. But he'd do so from the sidelines. Enjoy watching her discover the part of her soul she was eager to find.

CHAPTER TWO

J osie couldn't breathe. Unable to move. What would happen now? A stranger was going to do God knew what with her, and as much as she should be frightened, she had no fear. Arousal touched every part of her body.

His dark eyes held a note she'd never seen in a man before. More than confidence—he exuded arrogance.

"My rules are simple." His voice rumbled through the room and her breathing hitched. "From here on out, you will answer me with yes or no."

She nodded, soon realizing she'd defied him, so followed up by saying, "Yes." To her surprise she shifted on her feet and felt wetness in her panties. Could she be aroused already? *Apparently so.*

"For tonight we will use the safeword, *Castillo.*" He went on, "At any point if you cannot handle what I give to you, use the word and I will stop."

"Yes."

He stepped away from her, his intense gaze on hers, and she

felt his stare to the bottom of her toes. Heat rushed through her before it concentrated between her thighs.

"Undress."

The simple word should have made her uncomfortable. However, it didn't, not with his molten gaze on her, and the power held there. She'd come there for a reason. The lifestyle made her wet whenever she thought of it. All of which had to mean something, and she needed to discover why it turned her on so much.

With force, she pushed away any and all shyness, and removed her clothing until she stood in front of him, nude, her hands trembling a little.

He approached her again, stopped mere inches away and ran his finger over each of her breasts. "Stunning."

A little shiver rattled her and her breath whooshed out as the finger trailed over her taut nipple. His touch stayed a moment before he removed it and left her on display.

He strode over to the single rope on the floor, picked it up and came back toward her. Doubling the rope, he stepped in behind her and wrapped it around her neck so it dangled down to her legs. "This is about testing your limits. Awakening a part of yourself you never knew existed." He came to stand in front of her and tied the ends so the knot rested just above her breasts. "These bindings offer a way to free yourself. The ability to move is stolen from you, which heightens your other senses."

Josie's body burned. The heavy rope on her skin aroused her beyond measure. She hadn't known what he planned to do, but now with the nylon ties on her...nothing had ever felt so perfect.

"I'm going to push you." He made another knot resting just below her breasts. Then, he took the rope and wrapped it around her back where he tied a third knot. "You will be brought to a place where you are going to want to use your safeword, but restrain yourself. You're able to handle more than you think."

He brought the rope back to the front where he wrapped it first underneath her breasts, then above them.

She trembled. His touch so delicate and not at all what she expected from a Dom. Every deliberate wrap around her torso, and his undeniable skill, kicked her arousal up a notch.

As he wrapped it a final time under her breasts, he moved behind her again. There, he tied another knot between her shoulder blades. Bending, he took the other, smaller piece of twine and reached around to bind her wrists together.

By the time he'd finished, Josie's upper torso had been decorated by the rope. The inability to untie herself should have frightened her, considering it left her vulnerable to a man she knew nothing about. Yet, his soft touch, the tightness of the strands hugging her body, left her calm. Safe.

"Back up," he ordered.

She obeyed and he raised her hands above her head. She heard the snap of a clip, followed by the sensation of some of her weight transferred away from her feet. Glancing above her, she saw Gavin had clipped an obvious loop he'd made on her wrists to the rope that hung from the ceiling. She could still stand, however, as the anchor above her bore most of the weight.

Gavin ran his hand down her side to her hip, and Josie shuddered. He lifted her leg so the rope tied between the two poles rested between her thighs.

Without a word, he crossed the room where he'd left his bag. He reached down and pulled out three boxes. Josie's heart skipped a beat as his intention became clear. He held three vibrators, each with a large ball on the top and a handle resting below.

"These vibrators have not been used on another." His voice calm, so measured, telling her each step he took precise and planned out.

Josie didn't doubt it for a moment. No other man she'd met held his level of control.

After removing the vibrators from their boxes, he reached back into the bag and lifted out three smaller pieces of rope. He returned to Josie. He tied each of the vibrators onto the robe, equal width apart—a good couple feet between them.

Josie attempted to remain silent, not to make any kind of move, but as he continued to tie the vibrators onto the rope with skilled hands, she couldn't help herself. Eager moans fell from her lips as the heat quadrupled in her body, but his stern warning look shut her mouth with a loud snap.

Once he'd finished tying the last knot on the rope, he stood and approached her. His eyes lit with excitement and bore a promise of seduction. "You will listen to what I instruct you to do."

"Yes," she managed. Her pussy ached for the fun ahead. No foreplay had ever brought her to the level of desire she experienced at that moment. In fact, intercourse hadn't. The silky arousal between her thighs coated her heated flesh and she hadn't touched the vibrators yet. The implication of what he planned, the images in her mind, the way Gavin posed himself, the bonds around her skin, made her ready and eager for anything he offered her.

"If you do not do as I instruct, I will deliver a punishment." He tugged on the rope holding her in place as he tested the weight. "And you will pay for your defiance because I will enjoy delivering it."

He made his way to the vibrators. Leaning down, he turned each one on and Josie noticed they were set to varying speeds. Anticipation like no other burned in her pussy. In response, she squeezed her thighs together around her pulsing clit to ease the ache there.

"Release your legs," he growled.

Without thought, she opened her thighs and moaned in frustration as the pulse returned.

"I tell you when and how you can find your pleasure." She whimpered. His gaze scolded before he turned away, strode to the other side of the room and leaned against the wall. "Because of your disobedience you may move onto the first vibrator, count to five, then move off."

Josie sucked in a breath before she dared to inch forward. Two steps in, her pussy made contact with the low hum. A ping of pleasure rocketed through her and she gasped in elation. Yet, she wasn't about to disregard his instructions. She counted to five, before stepping away.

"Count to ten and move back on it."

Ten seconds had never felt so long. Her pussy clenched, the wetness along her skin creating a demanding need to gain relief. But she suspected it'd be a long time before she found her release. In truth, she wasn't quite sure how she'd get it. Would he step behind her and fuck her to find his own pleasure? She knew enough about the BDSM lifestyle to understand it had nothing to do with sexual gratification, but more so the journey to push ones limits further than anyone could imagine.

After she counted to ten, she stepped forward again, positioned herself on the vibrator so it connected to her clit. Her moans were impossible to hold in. She'd used vibrators before, but this one, even at the low setting, felt far more powerful than she'd ever experienced.

Her breasts were cupped by the ropes which increased the sensation, as if supporting her upper body. Her arms bound above her, she clenched her fists as the vibration excited her clit.

Gavin's voice lowered an octave. "Move off it."

Josie gasped out a long, deep breath and stepped back, starved of the wonderful feeling. It took a moment to catch her breath. Her legs trembled beneath her as the pleasure grabbed her.

Gavin approached and stood in front of her, watching her with intense eyes. "Now, move on it again."

Wiggling her way forward, she reached the vibration and lost her breath. The vibrations tickled, her only response quiet gasps.

"Move to the next."

If the low vibration aroused her, she anticipated what awaited her at the next level and her heart rate kicked up a notch. She reached the next vibrator and placed her clit upon it, shouting out against the hard hum along her sensitive flesh. Her head fell forward as she groaned. She squirmed a little and slid off the vibrator.

"Back on it," Gavin warned.

Not wanting to disappoint him, she responded to his demand and pushed her hips forward so the toy connected with skin. "Oh God," she shouted, her whole body quivering. Her head moved from side to side, her legs trembling beneath her as the sensations hurt. She fought against the urge to step away and give herself a moment to breathe.

"Look at me."

Josie gasped out as she raised her head. Her vision had hazed. Gavin appeared more of a figure than an actual man. Another ping of heat erupted with the vibration and she cried out.

"Take a deep breath," he ordered, his tone controlled, yet Josie heard the emotion behind his words. Clearly, he enjoyed watching her.

She listened and breathed.

"Calm down." His deep voice soft, sweet and appreciative.

The moment he said the order, she eased. He stood, powerful, his dark eyes stared intently in hers. It gave her strength and she pushed away the madness stealing her thoughts to focus on him. Soon, her vision cleared.

She sighed deep, tears dripping from the corners of her eyes as the intensity of her pleasure soared. Yet, she still held control. He guided her. Her pleasure lay in his hands and she gave him her body.

CHAPTER THREE

Gavin had done this same scene numerous times over. But never, in all his years, had he witnessed a sub give herself completely. In truth, all the subs before Josie had already been into the lifestyle—were already submissive to Doms.

His cock strained against his pants. Not only because she was a stunning woman, bound with the ropes he'd applied, finding intense pleasure, but for the first time ever, he'd found his submissive.

She shook as the vibrator pleasured her. Any moment she'd find her climax. Although when he told her to calm, she did so in an instant. She enthralled him.

Josie held his gaze, stood as firm in her stance as possible. Her jaw clenched tight to hold strong, even as her legs shook beneath her. He needed to push her. Test her limits to see if she'd pull out her safeword.

He took the few steps he needed to reach her, knelt down. "Do not take your eyes off me." He latched onto the vibrator and pushed it against her clit.

Her eyes went wide before they rolled back into her head. Just as fast as they did, they returned to meet his.

Very good.

He rolled the vibrator around to play along her clit. To stimulate her to a point where pleasure hurt. A small moan escaped her. He would put a stop to that. "Make a sound again and I will turn it off and make you wait."

She sucked her bottom lip and bit down. Clearly, not ready for her pleasure to end. Again, he admired her control. She had no idea how easily she fell into the role.

Any command he issued she followed. She blew his fucking mind.

Just as his mouth parted to offer another demand, she whispered, "May I come?"

Anger roared through him. He had not given her permission to speak. Although the request showed the submissive nature in her, it didn't mean he'd give her what she wanted. She had defied him. "No, you may not. Now step back."

With shaky legs, she raised her hips, shifted away from the vibrator. Her arousal coated the shiny plastic. Not good enough. He wanted to see the vibrator dripping.

Her legs wobbled, her breathing more erratic. He could have drawn the night out for hours if he wanted to. The knowledge she'd never done a scene before weighed heavy on his mind. The first experience would be intense for her, but she had already shown him the ability of perseverance. He craved to see how far he could push her.

Moving forward, he'd grant her the release she sought, only because he wanted her to go a step farther. He needed the orgasm out of the way before he did so. "Move back on it now. You are allowed to close your eyes and enjoy your climax."

Her cry escaped her, her trembling intensified as she shifted forward. She raised her hips and found the vibrator again. The second she did, she squealed, moaned, but held her body in place.

Gavin stared in complete awe. She released control, and he witnessed the pleasure rise to her face by her flushed cheeks. With her arms bound above her, she leaned forward, allowing the weight of the rope to hold her.

As he expected, her climax rose. She cried out and panted as she squirmed over top of the vibrator. Her mouth hung open as her head dropped, her body suspended, the exact reason he'd chosen to add the support of the ropes.

He allowed her to ride out her climax, enjoyed it himself. As she cried louder, her body froze, he waited by her side. Relished watching her find the release she sought.

The second her feet gave out on her, he latched onto her hips and shifted her off the vibrator. Beneath his hands her climax continued. Her body twitched and quivered in satisfaction.

A moment later, she raised her head and sighed. It amused him, though he understood. For Josie, an orgasm meant the end. He needed to teach her, show her what she'd experienced had been a tiny part of what her body *could* experience.

"Take a few breaths," he instructed. She fought for air and the last thing he needed was her to pass out. He required her to be aware.

Her mouth hadn't closed and her eyes were filled with pleasure. He wanted to drop his pants, grab hold of her slender frame and fuck her. His wants, though, didn't matter. The journey was about her. His duty to show her what she would gain as a submissive and how it could add to her life and her happiness.

When her breathing settled, he dropped his hands. "Move onto the next one." She made a tsk of disapproval. He frowned.

"I have not said you can have a break. Get on it. Now."

As she wiggled forward, she grunted in disbelief. Yet, she went, positioning herself on the vibrator with the highest speed. Pride filled him.

He held back his own groan. The second her skin connected, she screamed out and her head fell backward, before it whipped from side to side. Just delivered a climax, he knew she'd be beyond sensitive. And he also understood the sensations she felt now would not be pleasurable.

"Fuck," she cried.

He didn't begrudge her the right to yell out. His instructions were for her to answer him with yes and no responses to his questions. He recognized her need to roar against such intensity. His gaze stayed on her pussy as he witnessed the hard vibrations against her skin. She cried out again. No longer sounds of pleasure, but shrieks of pain. The speed of the vibrator shocked her system as he'd intended.

Leaving her where she stood, Gavin retreated against the wall to watch his prize. With her eyes wide open, tension filled her face as she strained against the ropes which bound her. His gaze traveled to her hands where she balled them into fists.

"Oh...God...." Her voice sounded tight through gritted teeth as she fought against the pleasure forced upon her.

Gavin reached down, adjusted his cock and stroked it twice. After the scene concluded, he planned to jerk off with the image of her submission in his mind. He studied her, deciding what she needed. This thing she sought out, the missing part of her life proved her to be a natural submissive. And he set out to prove it to her.

He called out, "Step away."

She fumbled but did obey. The earlier quivers gave way to a full out quake, her breathing so short and deep, she needed a break to gather herself. He would not let her come down from the rising climax.

"On it," he ordered.

She placed her splendid pussy back over top of the vibrator and screamed out as her head continued to move back and forth. So close, yet she couldn't find it.

The exact acknowledgement Gavin needed. Josie was a perfect submissive—she'd never find it on her own.

Her screams poured around him, a clear sign of complete loss of control, the sound strengthening his already hard cock. The pleasure she found was of the most brutal kind. He knew once this ended, she'd yearn to return.

Pushing off the wall, he approached her. She needed guidance. Her current state had begun to overwhelm her and he needed to intervene, or she'd break in front of him. Never his intention.

He ran his hands over her breasts and noticed they were soaked with sweat. As his touch connected, her body shook more and she sobbed. Begging for an end yet still pleading for it to continue.

He tweaked a nipple between his fingers, pinching it to shift her focus and bring her mind back to the present. "Look at me."

She raised her head, her eyes wild with both pleasure and pain. Her screams echoed through the room.

"Breathe."

The deep intake of breath did nothing for her agitated state. Her pretty eyes were crazed. He reached up, grabbed her chin and held her face in his firm grip.

"Breathe."

Trying to obey, she stifled a scream. Again and again, his admiration of her solidified as he watched her gather herself. She pushed past the pain, ignored the rough sensations tormenting her, and focused on his eyes. Acceptance was all he found.

Pure submission.

As much as it pleased him, it compelled him to push her further. She'd proven her ability to handle everything he'd made her do, especially for a newbie. He hadn't expected that. Not once had she pulled out her safeword. Telling him she could handle more.

He reached down to the vibrator, flicked the switch to increase the speed. A loud cry spilled for her lips as a deep shudder ran through her.

Yes, Josie, you are ready.

"Now, you may come," was all he said, before he stepped back to marvel.

Josie screeched out, the sound piercing. Her body convulsed, strained against the rope above her. Her skin flushed to a dark pink and Gavin had no doubt where the ropes dug into her skin, bruises would be left in their wake.

His eyes stayed trained on her. She could step away, move off the vibrator to end it, but she didn't. She stayed, fought through the meaning of her right and wrong, her definition of what pleasure meant, because he asked it of her. She didn't only impress him, she captivated his soul.

As her cries grew louder and tears fell, he expected she would stop and use her safeword. But as the minutes passed, she never did. She separated from herself. Gave into the sensations offered and rode it like a pro.

Her screams melted together. She teetered on the brink of her climax, yet unable to reach it. Gavin understood he needed to intervene to push her over the edge. He knelt down before her and knew she'd have no idea he stayed there, as lost as she was in the experience.

Reaching out, he latched onto the vibrator, his other hand came up to her hip to steady her. He pressed it against her clit. She screeched as though he'd cut off a limb. He applied pressure and circled the toy around her little nub and she convulsed harder.

The noises from her mouth were cries, nothing that would appear erotic to most, but to him she sounded lovely. He continued on and heard the hitch in her breath.

He studied her face for a moment, her muscles bunched together as her legs stuck out and her toes curled. The exact reason he had bound her arms above her.

His gaze drifted to her pussy at the first signs of her release. Small droplets of liquid fell on his hand. He tightened the grip around her hip and pushed harder against her with the vibrator.

One last roar echoed from her throat before wet warmth washed down her thighs. He moved her hips off the vibrator as she hung from the ropes binding her. Her head fell forward, her soft whimpers sliding around him like a warm bath.

She would need his aftercare, and he would offer it. For now, he stared at her as she dangled from the ropes he'd provided.

His masterpiece.

Chapter Four

Josie blinked a few times. Clarity returned. She vaguely remembered Gavin assisting her off the harness, removing the ropes he had placed upon her and the burn in her muscles easeing from being stretched. As she squirmed, thick arms tightened around her. "Don't move."

Cradled in his arms, she released a long sigh of contentment and sank into him, waiting out the moment. Giving herself time to gain her thoughts again.

He held her tight and said nothing. As the moment passed, something swelled inside her. Something she'd never felt before.

Rightness.

Tears filled her eyes, but it seemed silly to cry in front of him so she tried to stop them with a deep sniff. Gavin forced her to look at him. "Don't be ashamed of your emotions. I expect you to have that reaction."

"You do?" Her voice sounded shaky, even to her.

A small smile lifted the corner of his mouth. "I would." He rubbed her arms, easing her sore muscles.

Josie tried to gain understanding of what had happened, but her mind was void. Only completion lived within her. Instead of trying to force herself, she voiced her confusion. "Why do I feel a little lost?"

"You lost yourself in your pain and pleasure."

Josie took a moment to remind herself of all the past events, remembering the woman who entered the hotel before Gavin. The emptiness held in her soul and the desire for something more. She'd found what she sought. More than the act of the climax, the pleasure which defined the experience as a life-altering moment, it was her role. The need to have someone else control her. The desire to kneel at Gavin's feet and respond to his every demand, and the want to push past what she thought capable.

She belonged there. With him, in that room, under his command.

Her hunt to discover something she thought she needed, craved. It had nothing to do with her. Nothing she needed to find. She couldn't find happiness because happiness had to be given to her. Told to her. Shown to her. Controlled by another.

By Gavin.

But what did he want? He held her as if he cared for her, but normal protocol called for caring for the submissive after a scene. Did it explain why she experienced an attachment to him? The need to be his. Maybe? All she knew was she had found her happiness. In him. And she never wanted to let it go.

"Did you enjoy your experience?" His voice comforted her as it drew her away from her thoughts.

"I enjoyed it immensely." She laughed.

His eyebrow arched. "Do you have any questions?"

Did she? Her mind felt clearer now, and lots of things captured her thoughts. Only one stood out as most important to her. A question she needed answered to settle some of the emotions she felt now. "Am I good at it?"

The arch of his brow fell as a serious look crossed his face. "You belong in this role."

The confirmation she needed. In her soul, being submissive, always wanting to satisfy, to not disappoint came as a natural response for her. Before she thought it just a part of her character and why she excelled in most areas of her life. Now however, she believed it almost a shame she'd wasted it on people who didn't deserve her kindness. There was only one person she wanted to offer such gratitude to, which brought another question to her mind. "Is it always like this?"

"Like what?"

She squirmed a little in his arms, uncomfortable about the subject matter, but he held her firm in his grip. Resolved he'd answer honestly and not judge her, she continued. "I feel quite attached to you."

A little twinkle rose in his eyes. "A Dom and sub always have a strong connection. The journey together causes the intense reaction."

Her heart sank at his words. She experienced these feelings because of the event, a normal feeling to occur. Part of her had hoped they shared something unique. Something special between them. "Oh." Disappointment made her mutter the response.

Gavin smiled a delectable grin. "What we experienced tonight, however, what you showed me, the responses you gave...it's deeper than anything I have ever experienced before."

She gasped as she stared into his eyes. Such truths lay in their depths. Elation stole her sanity and touched her soul. Had he declared something more lived between them? Had he felt it, too? She wanted to believe it with every ounce of her being.

She'd walked into the room earlier, a woman filled with wishes and wants. But who remained now, someone entirely different. In Gavin's arms, comforted by his strong hold, her hopes and dreams could be built.

♋

Duty called for aftercare of a sub. Cuddling one until they made sense out of their experience, to allow them to be comfortable leaving the scene created just for them.

Now though, he didn't care for her out of obligation. The moment had everything to do with Josie. He yearned for a submissive he felt worthy of dominating. One who stirred him as much as he did her—someone who pushed past her limits because he demanded it. A sub who held the role not because of a choice, but because it'd been born into her.

Josie.

He brushed her hair away from sweat-drenched skin. She appeared confused, still processing everything she'd gone through. His eagerness however, made it impossible to wait. For the first time in his life, he felt out of control, as if his future depended on another.

She recognized the connection between them, and the acknowledgment sent a thrill coursing through his blood. He wouldn't let her walk out without him. If he had to sway her, he would do whatever he had to. Yet, her soft spoken words, her little admission that she held an interest in him, declared he didn't need to. He wouldn't waste the moment by beating around the bush, and set out to stake his claim. "I want to keep you."

"Pardon?" she squeaked, her eyes filled with shock.

It didn't surprise him to see she had a hard time processing

78

what he'd said. He had trouble believing it himself, but he had his chance and was going to take it, full throttle. "When we arranged tonight through Madame Eve, I must admit I doubted anything would come of it. I realize the experience had been arranged to welcome you into the lifestyle—to test it out to see if it appealed to you. But what I saw of you tonight tells me you are a special submissive. One I want to give everything I have to offer as a Dom, and more."

Tears rimmed her stunning blue eyes and he saw happiness in them. It occurred to him then she doubted what he felt toward her. She had given him something special, something he had long searched for. He wasn't going to hold back and not share his thoughts with her. "You are the first woman who has outlasted me."

Her shock returned. "I am?"

He nodded and hoped his expression showed his pride. "You didn't once use your safeword." He still had difficulty accepting that truth. Women who had been in the lifestyle for years always pulled it out because he pushed them beyond their limits. Josie never cracked. It's what fuelled his desires. "I'm not sure I can explain to you what this experience tonight meant for me."

"Try to...." Her tone sounded eager and he knew part of it was because she needed reassurance and acceptance. He wouldn't deny her.

He took a moment to ponder it all to make sure he got his words right. After a lingering moment, he gathered his thoughts enough to be sure he made sense. "The feeling you have right now, the one which says you are fulfilled and you have pleased someone else beyond measure—I have never experienced such a feeling."

Her eyes widened. "Ever?"

"No." He shook his head, finding her incredulousness

endearing. "I have been a Dom to many, some for a short time, some for longer, but I've never reached my climax of feeling satisfied. You have given me that tonight."

She smiled, and it warmed him. "Well, I'm glad to know I am not the only one who experienced a mind-blowingly satisfying moment tonight."

He chuckled.

She leaned forward, her lips coming so close to his. "Are you giving me a choice?" Her playful tone sparked an attraction to both her submissive side, and her personality as well. "Doesn't that go against the grain, so to speak?"

He understood why she'd carry those thoughts. She was new to the lifestyle and she didn't have a full understanding of what that lifestyle entailed. He needed to set her straight. "In scenes, we hold these roles. In life, I want you to have a voice."

"In life?" she repeated.

Clearly, she hadn't missed his intention. Yes, undeniably, he wanted to be her Dom. However, more lived within him. Something he never expected to find and something he suspected she felt, too. "I know this is all so sudden." He brushed his knuckles against her cheek. "But I'd like to get to know you better, not just as your Dom, but as a man, as well."

Her eyes filled with the same happiness in his own heart before she smiled in the most darling of ways. "I'd like that too."

Joy filled him as he closed the distance to capture her lips. Her kisses were just as he expected, soft and submissive.

The night may have been a matchmaking provided by Madame Eve, but now much more existed here. His heart warmed at the thought of showing her more, teaching her things she couldn't even think herself capable of, and sinking his cock into her sweet body.

He'd never dreamed of experiencing love at first sight, the

possibility of a soul mate, yet he'd just been proven wrong. He'd found her.

His submissive—forever bound.

TAKEDOWN

BY

STACEY KENNEDY

CHAPTER ONE

Wyatt stretched in the leather seat of his rented truck. A week of chasing Katrina Whittaker had brought nothing but dead ends. His team of U.S. Marshals were strategically positioned at different hotspots in Turks and Caicos, yet the search resulted in them running in circles. She'd proven to be smart and didn't stay in one place long.

A murder in Houston, Texas resulted in a warrant for her arrest, and it was Wyatt's job as Chief Deputy U.S. Marshal to bring Katrina home. Unfortunately, he couldn't locate her. She had family in Turks and Caicos, and Wyatt's team got word she'd fled the day her warrant had been issued. Wyatt still tried to understand how she'd made it to the Caribbean island without her passport or the ability to board an airplane, but he'd been in this game long enough to know anything was possible.

Releasing a long deep sigh, Wyatt ran his hand over his tired face. Katrina had gotten under his skin and he couldn't wait to slap handcuffs on her. Day and night, they'd set up surveillance and staked out possible leads. The damn woman wasn't anywhere to be found. He glanced at the clock on the dashboard. *Ten o'clock.* Where had the day gone? He'd sat in this seat for well over twelve hours. His ass hurt, his legs tingled with pins and needles, and he needed sleep. More than ready for this to be over, he grabbed his cell phone from the cup holder and held the button on the side to initiate a radio single. "Wyatt to Taryn."

"Whatcha got, Chief?" Taryn Kincaid, his right hand woman, responded. Always ready and eager for the hunt ahead, he'd promoted her to Supervisory Deputy U.S. Marshal not long ago because of her exemplary work.

"Jackshit," he grumbled. "You?"

"Nothing here either, Sir."

Wyatt scanned the area, the luxurious condominiums located on the beachfront known to be Katrina's grandmother's house. Nothing stirred, except a cat or two crossing the street on a hunt for dinner.

His team, Taryn plus the four other deputies she resided over, had slept in their trucks only about ten hours the whole week and he felt the weight of it. He pushed hard in the beginning of the investigation to put heat on Katrina, leaving her nowhere to hide. The idea flopped. His team needed rest, as did he. "Go back to the hotel, check in, and we'll gather back up at seven hundred hours and start again."

"Ten four."

The hum of the radio cut off to silence. Starting the engine, Wyatt shot a final look toward the condominium, nothing to indicate Katrina had been there. He put the truck in drive and drove off, spying lush greenery around him.

Turks and Caicos was a quiet island and Wyatt expected as much. Most along the stunning beachfront properties were tourists looking for some peace. He wouldn't mind some time off himself. He loved his job, lived for the hunt, but a vacation sounded all too good. Long hours with little fun and he longed for more excitement than his present non-existent love life. So much in fact, he enlisted the services of 1NightStand, a match-making service out of Las Vegas, a few months back. He hoped Madame Eve would find a woman to fulfill his dreams since he'd yet to find one the traditional way.

Turning onto Grace Bay, Wyatt entered the main district of the island. Only a few minutes down the road, Castillo Hotels and Resorts appeared and he sighed in relief. The resort, like nothing he'd ever seen before with its Greek architecture, white textured walls and large pillars out the front. Spotlights beamed up from the ground to bask the building in a warm glow. Palm trees decorated the landscape, among many other tropical plants Wyatt couldn't identify.

At the main entrance, he stopped and put the truck in park as the valet attendant approached. Stepping out, Wyatt handed the keys to the attendant and in turn took a numbered ticket. "Let me grab my stuff before you head off." Turning on his heel, he strode toward the cab of the truck and grabbed his duffel bag.

He placed it on the ground to reach into his pocket, took out some cash and handed it to the attendant, who smiled in thanks before jumping into the driver's seat. As the truck pulled away, Wyatt made his way toward the resort, marveling at the structure. When he entered, the size of the building left him in awe. High ceilings, marble floors—owner Jackson Castillo hadn't held back when he built the resort. Once at the counter, Wyatt dropped his duffel bag and reached back to grab his wallet from his pocket to show his identification.

"Welcome to the Castillo Resort," the greeter said, happy as a clam. Her big brown eyes twinkled. Wyatt understood why she'd been chosen for the job. Her kind face made him feel welcome.

He read her name tag, *Susanne,* before glancing back up to her face. "Wyatt Tanning, checking in."

Susanne examined his ID for a moment before she glanced away and typed on her computer. "Ah, Mr. Castillo has given you the presidential suite for your stay."

Nice of him, but not needed. "That isn't necessary, any room will suffice."

"No, no," Susanne retorted. "Mr. Castillo's orders, I'm not given the liberty to disobey them." She handed him a key card. "We hope you have a wonderful stay here, Mr. Tanning. If you need anything at all, just pick up your phone and it will direct you to the front desk."

Wyatt took the card, placed it in his wallet and returned it to his back pocket. "As long as I have a bed, I'll be happy." He said it more to himself than to Susanne, and she didn't bother with his remark, instead moving on to the couple who approached the desk.

Newlyweds. The assumption not hard to come by, the pair couldn't keep their hands off each other, plus the gleaming new rings on their fingers were a dead giveaway. Wyatt wondered what such intense love would feel like, never having it, he had nothing to compare it to. He sighed away his pity and considered going up to his room to crash, but decided to get a drink first to wash away the frustrations of the hunt that went nowhere.

Picking up his duffle bag, he noticed neon lights flashing, *Bar,* across the way. He salivated at the thought of an ice cold beer and he strode into the bar without haste, pleased to find it not overly busy. An Ultimate Fighting Championship blared on the big screens placed around the room and most of the customers focused on that.

Perfect.

At the main bar, he pulled up a stool and sat. The bartender stood, fixing a drink for a woman at the other end and paid him no attention. Wyatt's focus though stayed trained on the bartender. Muscles layered muscles to create a sculpted physique leading him to believe the man worked out. Wyatt watched the bartender's forearm clench while he mixed the drink, and the sight of his toned body, tightened Wyatt's groin.

Wyatt might have a fondness for women, but it also extended to men, though that was one indulgence he never allowed himself. U.S. Marshal's did not get sexually involved with men. However, his hard cock reminded him his wish to ignore the draw to the same sex wasn't always possible.

The bartender looked up then gave a nod he'd be along shortly and Wyatt groaned. The man's face consisted of hard angles, sculpted features, buzzed, dirty blond hair with blue eyes exuding strength—it all appealed to him.

Ignoring his initial attraction, Wyatt focused on the wooden bar and took a deep breath to regain his sense of mind. His cock might want one thing, but his brain held strength over his body. He'd pushed away his cravings for years, become an expert at it. Resurrecting the wall of protection, he hid all emotion and demanded his cock behave.

The drink spilled over the rim of the glass as the ice clinked against the sides. Rye wiped the cloth against the bar to clean up the mess from the rum and Coke he'd prepared. He looked out to the bar, the hotel quite busy, considering the night was still early. The UFC fight gave energy to the room where shouts of encouragement rang out in loud outbursts. Two of the top fighters were in the third five-minute round with only two minutes remaining and if Rye had a chance to have a go at them, he'd jump on the opportunity.

The ring had been his home for the past decade of his thirty-four years. He excelled, won some championships, but not enough to get him in the ring with the likes of the pros. Not that he minded. His contentment lay in the life he led, he traveled to fight when he could, but moved to Turks and Caicos for the relaxing atmosphere. He settled into a fine life there a year back and did not intend to leave anytime soon.

After he cleaned up the remaining mess, he tossed the towel aside and approached the waiting customer. A U.S. Marshal. The badge on his hat declared so much and the words written in white block letters on the back of his navy tee-shirt confirmed it to be true.

Rye grinned. A law man sent his arousal into full alarm. The tough persona, the harsh personality, exactly the type of man Rye enjoyed bedding. His women he liked sweet, with a bit of sass in their personality. Men he wanted ragged and rough around the edges. More fun to play with. To some, he'd be considered a bisexual, one who enjoyed both a woman's pussy and a man's tight ass. He hated the label and left it at he enjoyed sex. All types.

He drew closer to the man and his muscles tightened as he wiped his hands on his jeans. The Marshal, represented precisely what he'd been looking for in a lover. So much so, he'd enlisted the services of Madame Eve to help him find it. The men he'd been involved with were either too soft, too giving, or couldn't stand up to his personality. He craved a man to go head to head with, equal in strength and demeanor, a fantasy he'd hungered for for years and never fulfilled.

As the thought rose, annoyance burned his blood. Madame Eve had yet to live up to her obligation. Months had passed and she hadn't found him what he sought. Pushing his irritation away, he stopped in front of the Marshal. "What's your pleasure?"

The Marshal raised his gaze and Rye bit back a groan. The man's occupation made him appealing, the hard exterior of his features captivated Rye. Russet hair peeked out beneath his baseball cap, curling up at the ends. His eyes rich as chocolate, and the chiseled manner of his jaw line and lips made Rye's cock heavy.

"Cold beer," Wyatt responded.

Rye cleared his throat before turning away to grab the beer from the fridge below the bar. He grabbed the bottle opener from his pocket, flicked it open and handed it him, brushing against his hand with his own. The man tensed before he raised the bottle to his mouth and took a long draw on it.

Was that a flicker of interest Rye witnessed at their touch? Intrigue held too much in his body not to find out. First, he'd play it cool. The Marshal might stir erotic thoughts, but Rye had enough sense to tell he looked exhausted. "Rough night?"

Wyatt lowered the beer from his mouth and wiped away the remaining liquid on his lips. "A rough week."

Rye noted the gravelly tone to his voice, due to tiredness or a given attribute, he couldn't be sure. Didn't much matter, he enjoyed it nonetheless. "That bad of a vacation is it?"

"No vacation." Wyatt shook his head, spinning the beer bottle in his hand. "On a case."

Interesting.

Rye's curiosity peaked, needing to become better acquainted with the Marshal, he offered his hand. "Rye Daniels."

"Wyatt Tanning." He wiped his hand on his shirt before he shook Rye's.

Again, a flash of interest appeared on the Marshal's face at the contact. Rye had enough experience to know straight-men, but he doubted the man before him only enjoyed the likes of women. Remaining blasé, he continued with the small talk. "I take it you haven't found whoever you're looking for."

"Nah." Wyatt took another long sip of his beer. His lips made a suction sound as he lowered the beer back down and Rye stifled the moan threatening to escape his lips. "Not even close."

Rye leaned against the counter, brought his gaze back to Wyatt's, and took notice of something when he did. The Marshal's gaze drifted to his forearm, which Rye could feel had flexed with the move. His eyes widened slightly and his breath drew in deep, before he clamped up.

To be sure he saw it right, Rye shifted positions repeating the move and Wyatt's eyes burned again, however, ceased an instant later.

A challenge.

Rye's adrenaline kicked up and his cock stiffened. To explore more, he reached down and shifted his erection in his pants and Wyatt tensed. His gaze snapped away and he drank his beer with his eyes focused on the bar ahead. It appeared the Marshal took notice of Rye as well, yet wasn't so inclined to indulge in such attractions.

Too bad for him, Rye lived to push limits. An opportunity had fallen into his lap. A dream come true, really. Not only did it provide the exact type of man Rye longed for, but Wyatt had dared him not to try, even if he hadn't meant to. Bored with the meaningless conversation, Rye tested Wyatt. "Got any plans for tonight?"

Wyatt's beer came down on the bar with a heavy thud. His eyes wide with surprise, but he hid it well a quick second later. "Early start tomorrow, my plans are to hit the sack and in the mornin' catch a killer."

The answer didn't surprise Rye. If anything, it pleased him.

Increasing the challenge only built the burn in his groin. "The Marshal gets no fun then?"

Wyatt cleared his throat, before he finished off his beer and stood. Reaching back into his pocket, he took out his wallet, grabbed a ten dollar bill and threw it on the bar. "Appreciate the beer, a good night to you."

Rye nodded in response and watched Wyatt leave, focusing on his tight ass filling his jeans. Wicked images played on his mind. That is, until he got interrupted.

"I'm here," Saul gasped, breathless.

"About damn time," Rye exclaimed, glancing toward one of the other bartenders at the hotel. "You're an hour late." Not that he minded. If he'd left when his shift ended, he would've missed the Marshal.

"Sorry, got stuck on a call with an old friend." Saul looked away when a customer approached the bar. "Go on, I've got it handled now."

Rye pulled twenty bucks from his pocket, placed it in the cash register and helped himself to a six pack of beer from the fridge. Good thing Susanne at the front desk adored him because he needed to know one thing—Wyatt's room number.

Chapter Two

At room two-twelve, Wyatt slid the keycard into the door and after the beep, yanked the door open and slammed it behind him. His full cock hadn't stopped reminding him he'd found the bartender sexy as sin. Yet, the voice in his mind told him U.S. Marshals didn't indulge in such activities.

He'd fight these feelings just as he'd fought them for the length of his thirty-five years. He never thought of himself as a homosexual man since women held as much appeal to him. In truth, he hoped to find himself married to a woman who would bear his child at some point. Nevertheless, he couldn't ignore the lust he carried for men, the want to be buried balls deep in a tight ass or have a man sucking him off.

Again though, he reminded himself, U.S. Marshals shouldn't want such fantasies met. He'd spent years battling against his desires, knowing it was more important for him to find a wife and marry as society called for. However, his body always disagreed with him.

He tossed the keycard down on the dresser and admired the

space before him. His team stayed at the Castillo Resorts and Hotels alongside him. Jackson Castillo, owner of the resorts, gave them no trouble while on a case. If anything, had offered them many bonuses most hotels didn't give. The department paid next to nothing for the rooms here, which pleased him. The last thing he needed was the Director of the U.S. Marshals Service coming down on him for high travel costs.

Really though, he wasn't used to such luxury. The suite Jackson arranged for him looked more like an apartment than a hotel room. Two plush couches surrounded a fireplace with a big screen television above. To the right, the bedroom had a four-poster king size bed and rich bedding. To the left, a fully stocked kitchen, larger than the one Wyatt had back at his home in Houston.

Plopping onto one of the couches, he pulled off his cowboy boot. As he slipped the other off his foot, a loud knock came at the door. He wasn't expecting any visitors and he doubted his team would contact him by a simple knock. They knew they needed to call ahead before they interrupted him off duty.

Wyatt approached the door, looked through the peep hole and surprise made him take a step back. Of all the scenarios in his mind of who it could be, this had not been one of them. Curious, he opened it.

The bartender stood, a six pack in hand and a grin on his face. "Thought you might need another one."

Wyatt glanced down the hallway, relieved to find it bare. His heart skipped a beat. What he didn't need was his team seeing a man at his door holding beers. Rye didn't look like a bellboy and Wyatt didn't want the implication of where minds could take the situation.

Resolved to get him in before anyone saw, and to ascertain what his appearance was all about, Wyatt opened the door wider. "Come on in."

Rye stepped through the threshold and Wyatt gave another look down the hall for good measure. Glad to see quiet halls before him, he shut the door and turned back to Rye, who examined the room.

He whistled. "Some place."

Rye's reply stunned Wyatt. Being a bartender at the resort, he'd expect the man to be aware of what the hotel held. "You've never been in the suite before?"

"Never needed to be." Rye spun on his heels, heading toward the kitchen.

Wyatt took a seat on the couch, curious as to the reasons behind Rye's visit. He hadn't offered an invitation, nor gave any indication he wanted him there. Rye rummaged around the kitchen, depositing the beer into the fridge. Seconds passed before he returned with two opened beers and handed one to him. Wyatt took the cold beer and drank a few gulps, studying Rye as he sat on the opposite couch.

Many moments passed before Wyatt grew tired of the staring contest and wanted Rye to leave. Something about all this made him feel uncomfortable. The look in Rye's eye, the determined set of his expression, he needed this man to go. "Thank you for the beer. I appreciate the gesture." He stood and strode to the door about ready to open it when a firm hand grasped his bicep.

"I'm not going anywhere."

Wyatt first glanced at the hand holding strong around his arm then looked to Rye. His defenses skyrocketed. He shoved the man's hand off and stepped away. "Not sure you're given a choice."

Rye closed the distance between them, coming face to face with him. Wyatt couldn't help but respect the tenacity the man carried. No one stood up to him. Yet, for him, the closeness sent a hot wave of panic to course through his veins. Whatever Rye was after, he didn't want. "Move away from me. Now." He gave him a steady push and Rye stumbled back on his feet.

Wyatt witnessed a flash of a challenge form on Rye's face and anger roared within him, fully understanding the reasons behind his visit. "I have no interest in whatever you came here for."

Rye arched an eyebrow. "Don't you?"

Words were lost to Wyatt now as the truth stared at him with deep blue eyes. Confronted, cornered, a position he didn't like. Doing the only thing he could think of, he slugged Rye across the jaw and he went down like a sack of potatoes.

Rye opened his jaw to stretch out the muscles. He hadn't expected the hit, nor prepared for it. The challenge increased. Adrenaline spiked in his body and arousal tore through him. He wanted Wyatt and he wouldn't take no for an answer. Pouncing off the floor, he plowed into Wyatt to send them smashing back into the wall. A loud crack declared they'd just dented the plaster.

Wyatt didn't flinch. He shot back by pushing Rye onto the ground and squeezing his thighs around his waist, pinning his shoulders to the ground in an attempt to hold him there. "Stay where you are. Do you have any idea who I am?"

"Don't know, don't care." Rye thrust underneath with his hips to release the hold and the pressure eased enough to allow him to rise back up on his knees. He shoved with all his might, sending Wyatt back and then flipped him over so they reversed positions.

With Wyatt face down, Rye placed his knee on his back, using all his weight to pin him. His left leg stretched out beside him to maintain his balance in a move learned long ago through UFC training.

As expected, Wyatt flung his arm back to get a hit, but Rye was ready, grabbed him behind the elbow, trapping his arm behind him making him defenseless. Wyatt grunted, sounding both annoyed and in pain.

"Do you yield?" Rye's voice sounded through clenched teeth, using all his strength to hold Wyatt to the ground. Wyatt held more power than some of the fighters he'd gone up against. Didn't much surprise him, the man was a U.S. Marshal, the job demanding he stay fit.

"You do realize, I have a gun strapped to my waist," Wyatt sneered. "And you have just physically attacked a U.S. Marshal."

Rye's gaze flickered to the gun in the holster—the weapon didn't bother him. If anything it gave strength to the hard-on he'd suffered from during the wrestling match. "Self-defense as I see it. You attacked first, and give it a couple hours, I'll have the shiner to prove it."

After a long pause, Wyatt sighed. "Fine, I yield. Get the fuck off."

Rye grinned as he shifted, released Wyatt's arm and allowed him out of the hold. He stood, unaware when Wyatt lunged at him, weapon drawn. They tumbled to the ground with the gun pointed at Rye's chest.

"What game are you playing?" Wyatt accused.

"No game." Rye's nerves didn't falter. He held no concern over the weapon pointed at him. Wyatt would never shoot. Any man given the role he held as a Marshal rose to that position by hard work and honor. "You planted the seed. I'm here to water it."

Wyatt blinked, before his eyes narrowed. "What seed did I plant?"

"You think I didn't see the *fuck-me eyes* you gave me downstairs? The way you watched my body and the look you got when you saw me touch my cock?"

"I-I-didn't...." Wyatt pulled the weapon back, holstered it and stood to put some distance between them. Before he did, Rye felt Wyatt's hardened bulge resting against his thigh.

The Marshal might be in denial, but his body wasn't. Rye jumped to his feet and squared his shoulders. "Denial must be such a luxury."

Wyatt snorted. "Meaning?"

A thousand meanings, Rye thought. What good would it do to explain? The Marshal would make some random excuse and deny it all to hell. Rye had enough pussyfooting around. His needy cock demanded attention. "I know you want me, your eyes cannot lie and your hard cock proves it." He grasped onto the hem of his T-shirt and flung it over his head. Then he stood, bare-chested. Arousal crossed Wyatt's face. It didn't surprise him. A UFC fighter for well over ten years, Rye's body was in impeccable shape and stirred many reactions just like the one he witnessed now. What interested him more was the body under Wyatt's cotton T-shirt. He didn't need to look hard to see toned thighs beneath his jeans, and furthermore, the heavy treat that Rye felt before. If he judged right, Wyatt's cock was thick and long and he wanted to get a hold of it.

Taking a step toward him, Wyatt didn't move away, his gaze intent on Rye's approach, his jaw working, clenching the muscles there.

Once in front of him, Wyatt cleared his throat. "I'm not gay."

"Nor am I." Rye's response seemed to startle Wyatt. His expression became perplexed, before he could get ahead of himself, Rye answered his unasked question. "I like sex, all types of sex, with all types of lovers." He reached out and cupped Wyatt's cock, stroking the rock hard erection. "Tonight I want this. Other times, I want pussy. It doesn't make me anything other than a man who likes to indulge and is open to many kinds of pleasure."

Wyatt's eyes burned, seemed that Rye had thrown him a line to grab onto and showed they shared the same desires. At the same time however, confusion washed across Wyatt's expression. They stood for long moments, staring, while Rye stroked Wyatt's cock. Either Wyatt came to a resolution in his mind or the pleasure he received decided for him since his apprehension melted away to hard desire. Not saying a word, Wyatt reached for his shirt and pulled it over his head.

Rye released his hand from Wyatt's cock, traveling it up to feel the hard planes of muscles beneath the soft, dark hair over Wyatt's body. Not enough hair to cover his square chest and tight abs, but enough it spiked Rye's arousal. He might have a smooth chest to show off the dragon tattoo that started at his pectoral muscles, ran over his shoulder and all the way down his back to his buttocks, but he liked his men...robust.

He ran his hands over Wyatt's hard muscles. Moving down, he traced the rippling edges of Wyatt's abs until his fingers trailed over the belt buckle. He dropped his hand into the rim of Wyatt's pants, raised his gaze and yanked him forward.

"Tell me...." Rye stared into Wyatt's eyes, challenging him to say no now.

A wicked glint appeared in Wyatt's eye before he pushed hard against Rye's chest until he hit the wall. His lips crushed against Rye's. Powerful. Kiss for kiss, dominance filled the air until it was thick with it.

Wyatt broke off the kiss and stepped back. His eyes hooded

and dark with desire, he kept his gaze on Rye as he began to unbuckle his belt and switched positions so he stood with his back to the wall. Moments later, his pants pooled at his feet.

"Get on your knees," Wyatt demanded.

Rye's cock throbbed, the order making his arousal sizzle. He reached down, freed his own erection from his pants to give himself pleasure, while he offered it to Wyatt, and knelt. Latching onto Wyatt's dick, he gave it a long steady stroke, pleased with what was before him. His assumptions weren't wrong, the man had been gifted with a spectacular cock.

Wyatt's head fell back and he moaned.

Rye grinned. He would enjoy sucking Wyatt off, giving him a pleasure he'd never known. Pleasure only found with a man's mouth and hand. Leaning forward, he inhaled the musty scent of Wyatt, parted his lips and had his first taste of a U.S. Marshal.

CHAPTER THREE

Wyatt's legs trembled beneath him. He pushed his back against the wall to steady himself. His balls drew up tight and his cock thickened as Rye's mouth swept over his shaft. Hard, long pulls, nothing he'd ever experienced from a woman's mouth. No hesitation in Rye's moves, determined suction while he took the full length of Wyatt's cock into his throat.

Rye held Wyatt's sac in his hand, squeezed his testicles to near pain, yet his muscles tensed at the sensation and pleasure soared through him. He groaned as Rye continued to draw on him.

After a languorous suck, Rye backed away, keeping hold at the base of Wyatt's cock and gave it a shake. "Nothing better than a man's mouth, is there?"

Wyatt lowered his head and his cock grew harder watching Rye kneel before him, offering himself. Rye's hand worked over the length of Wyatt with hard pressure. "Feels just as good as you jerking it."

Working Wyatt's cock, Rye went from the tip all the way the

base, his hand squeezed against the hold. Wyatt's jaw clenched, the pleasure forcing growls from his mouth and he widened his legs to stabilize himself. Rye never hurried his touches, never jerked him to come, only savored.

Releasing his hand around Wyatt's sac, Rye trailed his fingers underneath to the soft skin behind. Wyatt's head fell back against the wall with a loud bang. The touch on the sensitive spot stole his breath. Rye stroked his finger along in a come-hither motion while he continued to jerk him off.

Wyatt's leg trembled, pants echoed from his mouth, before Rye dropped his hand, stood and walked toward the nightstand. Known to cater to its clients well, Wyatt wasn't surprised at all when Rye opened the drawer to find the Castillo resort provided a bottle of lubrication. He unsealed the plastic wrap, applied the clear shiny liquid to his finger then returned to Wyatt.

Wyatt stood, cock standing out from his body, demanding more. Rye knelt again, placed his finger on the sensitive area, but moved further back this time. He pressed his finger against Wyatt's anus. His muscles trembled around the touch. No one had ever touched his sweet spot before and Wyatt lost his mind.

"A virgin ass," Rye groaned, "My favorite kind." He dipped his finger through the tight knot of muscles.

Wyatt vibrated. "Fuck."

While Rye worked his finger, he brought his mouth back to the tip of Wyatt's dick and sucked. Wyatt's only recourse, grab the man by the head and demand he take more. Ruthlessly, Wyatt fucked his mouth. Rye buried his finger deep in his ass and the sensation made Wyatt's eyes roll back into his head as Rye's finger played with his prostate.

Rye continued to stroke, forcing Wyatt to look back to him, his hand moving fast over Wyatt's shaft, his eyes staying focused on Wyatt as his mouth welcomed him. Wyatt's cock hit the back of Rye's throat, yet he took it, moved past the gags that came in protest and owned that moment.

Fuck yeah!

With the sight of Rye before him, the sensations stole all train of thought from his mind, and Wyatt's climax rose. The need to spill captured him, however he didn't want it to end. No, he needed to make this moment last as long as possible. Raising his leg, he pushed against Rye's chest sending him back on his ass. His finger yanked from the home it found. "Come here."

The grin on Rye's face declared he didn't mind the change in positions. Wyatt reached down, latched onto Rye's arm and tugged him up. He pressed his body against Rye's, feeling his cock connect with his. He rolled his hips to rub himself along Rye, and he mirrored it. Thrusting against him, Wyatt took his mouth in a hard kiss. Tongues crashed. Lips crushed. Cocks rubbed together. Heat burned like wildfire through his body.

Wyatt grunted against his lips, his cock throbbing for more, pulsating to be freed from the pleasure it suffered. Yet, he held other interests. He'd been sucked, and sucked beyond measure. Never having his lips on a man's cock, Wyatt's mouth watered to experience Rye's taste. Feel Rye's large cock hit his throat as Rye found his own pleasure.

Breaking away from the kiss, he pushed Rye back until they entered the bedroom and Rye's thighs hit the bed. Wyatt gave him another steady shove until Rye fell back on the bed, legs dangling off the edge. Wyatt latched onto his open jeans, yanking them off and throwing them aside. He kicked Rye's legs wide open and stepped between them, grasping his needy cock.

Rye moaned.

Wyatt marveled at the man's engorged length. He'd always wanted to experience this, dreamed of this moment, and here now, he wished he'd done this a long time ago. Nothing looked sexier. Hard lines of a thick body, not soft like a woman's a body. It brought him to a fevered pitch. He gripped the tip of Rye's cock and gave a steady squeeze, before running his hand down his shaft. Doing that, the feel of Rye, sent his arousal sky high.

Bending over him, Wyatt opened his mouth and devoured Rye. The salty taste of pre-cum titillated his taste buds as he tasted cock. He bobbed his head, working his mouth in a way he'd want for himself. Rye rocked his hips up in matching rhythm. Needing more, feeling the rush of his need, Wyatt gathered Rye's balls in his hands, holding them close to the base of his cock. Rye's groans of approval were deep, but not deep enough. Wyatt wanted to see the man who showed him this new type of pleasure writhing in desire.

He gave another steady suck before he released Rye from his mouth. His cock fell down to lay on his ripped abs. Wyatt licked his way down his shaft, to his testicles where he took each one into his mouth to play with, earning him low moans from the other man. Moving lower, he reached the soft skin Wyatt never knew possessed such intense nerve endings. He flicked it with his tongue and Rye's legs quivered, a guttural groan sounding from his mouth.

Pushing at Rye's thighs, he widened him, opened his ass for him and dipped his tongue along the little bud. Rye gasped, straightened up, his gaze focused on Wyatt's and he'd never seen such want in a pair of eyes. Rye grasped onto his cock, and began jerking it while Wyatt tickled his anus.

In response, Wyatt grabbed onto his own length and began stroking it to find his pleasure. Wyatt drew in deeper, applied more pressure with his tongue, and Rye panted, fell back on the bed while he stroked his cock with purposeful intent.

Wyatt's eyes shut as his cock hardened, his release on the brink. Forcing himself to calm, he dropped his hand to draw the moment out and brought his tongue back into his mouth, releasing Rye from the sensations gripping him.

Rye raised his head, arched an eyebrow with a deep flush to his cheeks. "You might have a virgin ass, but you suck cock like a pro." He shifted off the bed to turn onto his stomach, hips positioned on the edge with legs spread wide. "Now, let's see if that status applies to how you fuck."

Rye's heart raced in anticipation. Wyatt strode over to his pants, grabbed a condom out of his wallet and proceeded to apply it. He wanted to be buried in Wyatt's tight ass when he came, but he'd give Wyatt the first go, a new experience he wouldn't deny him.

Wyatt approached, a wanton burn in his eyes. He grabbed the lube off the night table, drenched his cock in it and put some on his hand. Standing between Rye's legs, he spread his ass cheeks with his hand and ran the liquid along Rye's bud. Keeping his cheeks spread apart, he pressed his cock against Rye's anus and inched his way in, allowing the muscles to relax to accept him.

"Tight," Wyatt grated.

Thoughts fled Rye's mind. An unforgiving lover, Wyatt thrust his hips forward, the muscles giving way to free moans from not only Wyatt, but Rye, too. Over and over again, he came at him with a steady pace, in and out, rendering Rye cross-eyed.

Rye's cock moved against the bed beneath him, only adding to the sensations building inside. His G-spot stimulated by Wyatt's hard cock, Rye grabbed onto the bed sheets and groaned in pleasure.

Wyatt gripped his ass, kept Rye's cheeks spread as he

delivered hard thrusts against his buttocks. Skin met skin. Sounds of satisfaction echoed through the room as the pressure in Rye built. Waves of pleasure caused his breath to hitch. If he could latch onto his cock and stroke it blindly, he'd come at any moment.

Since he couldn't, he let Wyatt's moves shift him back and forth on the bed to add to the sensation. His cock delighted, hardened further as it rubbed against the silk duvet.

"Fuck, so tight," Wyatt shouted, his thrusts taking on a new sense of urgency. His fingers dug into Rye's ass cheeks as he leaned more of his weight against him, thrusting harder.

The deep rasp of Wyatt's breath indicated his approaching climax. Rye tightened his ass, earning a raucous moan from the other man's mouth. Dropping his hands from his ass, he placed them on Rye's shoulders, pinning him.

Yes. Rye wanted this, craved to be used by a man of power.

Wyatt pushed harder against him and Rye's breathing hitched. The pressure on his lungs from Wyatt's hands forced his breath out in deep huffs. Wyatt showed him no mercy. He went at him as if it was his given right to fuck him senseless, and Rye marveled at the demand.

Sweat formed over Rye's body, and Wyatt's own perspiration dripped along Rye's back. A loud roar escaped Wyatt's throat with a final thrust that brought him deep into Rye's ass. Every muscle in Rye's body tightened and the extra stretch caused from Wyatt's widening erection made Rye mirror the roar. Wyatt's weight dropped down on Rye's back. He trembled, groaning out as his cock spilled.

After his shuddering ceased, Wyatt moaned. "Fucking incredible." He shifted off Rye, plopped down onto the bed, yanked off the condom and threw it in the trash.

Rye steadied his breath, stood, his cock rock-hard and eager.

"You're about to eat your words. You've discovered nothing yet." He approached his jeans, took out a condom and wasted no time putting it on. Then, grabbed the lube to apply it on his cock and his hand. Once done, he glanced up to find Wyatt expectant for more. Soft from his release, his cock became semi-erect and building as Rye approached. Reaching out, Rye gave him a push to scoot to the center of the bed. "You didn't think you were the only one that got to enjoy an ass did you?"

No response came from Wyatt.

Rye settled in behind him, raised Wyatt's leg by hitching it on his arm and ran his hand over Wyatt's sweet ass to apply the lube, then brought his erection to where it craved to go. Gripping Wyatt's thigh, Rye pushed through the taut muscles. Wyatt groaned, and Rye assumed, some pain, some pleasure. His ass never fucked before, it needed preparation. Rye pushed in small increments, allowing him to be accepted.

His cock strangled by Wyatt's ass, Rye's only remedy from the pressure and the sensations threatening to make him explode was to lower his head back against the bed and moan out the pleasure of the moment. Inch by inch, Rye continued to push in until Wyatt accepted the full length of him, buried deep.

Wyatt's muscles relaxed, his body loosened and Rye tested the restraint by pulling out slightly to push back in. Tight—so incredibly tight—yet ready. Rye wouldn't waste a moment more. He needed to get off and he wanted to come now. "Prepare to get fucked."

Positioning himself up on his elbow, Rye wanted to watch Wyatt experience for the first time being taken in the ass, and without pause, he unleashed himself. Hard thrusts. Rough advances. Over and over again.

Rye had been close to coming before, now, he suspected in only moments he'd reach his end. His gaze lingered along

Wyatt's muscular body, so thick. Rye groaned witnessing the sheen of sweat making his skin look all that more appealing. It didn't surprise Rye in the least to find Wyatt's cock had hardened again, and to see he stroked it with dire need.

Pleasure demanded Rye to close his eyes and be lost to it. Yet, he couldn't stop looking at Wyatt. The intensity on his face. Lost to sensations as his ass got fucked, good and hard, for the first time. Instead, Rye stared, focused on Wyatt's expression and went wild, fuelled by a desire to make a claim on Wyatt.

Moans, grunts, groans filled the hotel room, the bed banging against the wall as Rye held nothing back. His own release built to extremes. He gripped Wyatt's leg tight against his body and roared against the pleasure building inside, his cock choked by Wyatt's tight rim.

Rye reluctantly closed his eyes as his balls drew up, his stomach clenched, and a wave of euphoria washed over him. He slammed hard against Wyatt's ass, buried balls deep, his cum pulsed from his cock, and as his own release delighted him, he opened his eyes to witness Wyatt's own release spill along his hand.

When the pleasure ceased, and Rye's sense of mind returned, he took a minute to catch his breath, leaning forward to nibble on Wyatt's nape, earning him a shiver. "Not only suck like a pro, but you fuck like one too, Marshal."

Wyatt chuckled, deep and throaty, glancing over his shoulder with a lustful gaze behind the exhaustion. "Give me a half an hour, and I'll prove to ya, you've only had a taste of how good I can fuck."

Rye, and his semi-hard cock, planned to hold him to that promise.

Chapter Four

Wyatt stirred from his slumber, sore in all the right places, when a stern voice called, "Taryn to Chief." He muttered a curse, rolling onto his side to grab the phone off the nightstand.

"Go ahead," he croaked.

"Headquarters just contacted me. Katrina's aunt informed us she has come to her home at Coral Gardens Beach Condominiums on Penns Road."

Wyatt sat up, the sheet sliding down his torso. Hearing the news didn't surprise him. When he arrived in Turks and Caicos, he'd come down hard on her family, even threatened to send them all to jail if he caught Katrina at their house. Her warrant involved a murder, so he suspected her family would hand her over if she popped her head up. And he'd been right. "Gather the team, I'll meet you at the location in twenty."

A quiet, *ahem*, captured his focus. Wyatt glanced over to find Rye with the sheet settled at his waist, giving him a fine view of muscles. His hands folded behind his head, he wore a sexy grin.

"Good mornin'."

"Mornin'." As his greeting ended, Wyatt noticed the black and blue bruise under Rye's left eye. Unhappiness filled him. "I've marked you there."

Rye raised his hand to his eye, pushed against the bruise and cringed. "So you did." He sat up, scooted close to Wyatt. "A little pain for pleasure never hurt anyone."

Rye's closeness stiffened Wyatt's cock and sent his heart racing. Rye closed the distance, took Wyatt's mouth with the force he expected from the man. Lips crushed against each other as tongues battled for dominance.

Wyatt's harsh groan sounded through a clenched jaw as he backed away. His hard-on made his thoughts revolve around the idea of his mouth wrapped around Rye's cock, being buried deep in his ass, experiencing this newfound pleasure. Yet, a job needed to be done. It would all have to wait. "I have to go."

"Duty calls?" Rye exhaled, flopping back onto the bed with his needy erection tenting the sheet.

Forcing his gaze away, Wyatt rasped, "Exactly." To confirm his thoughts, his phone beeped, indicating a text message awaited him. He stood, his cock standing erect from his body, demanding attention. Ignoring it, he reached for his phone just as Rye's cell beeped as well. He heard Rye grab his phone, however Wyatt's focus stayed on the message he read. His eyes had to be lying to him.

Sending a little follow-up message in hopes that you and Rye enjoyed your night together. I thank you for using 1NightStand to fulfill your match-making needs, and it's my wish that you found what you were looking for. Please remember, I will continue to strive to find the woman you have requested. For now, enjoy yourself.

Sincerely yours,
Madame Eve

Wyatt's mouth dropped open. He'd spent years alone, searching out the woman to make him happy, with no success. Two months ago, he'd enlisted the services of Madame Eve and filled out the questionnaire requesting to meet the woman of his dreams. Never did he expect to meet the man who'd freed him sexually and fulfill his buried fantasies. Furthermore, how in the hell did Madame Eve know deep down he craved to feel a hard masculine body? His suspicions rose and he wanted answers.

He snapped his accusing gaze to Rye. "Did you know of this?"

"I had no idea." Surprise widened Rye's eyes. He shook his head, his face blank with confusion. "I filled out a questionnaire for Madame Eve's services a while back, but she never contacted me to say she found a match. Nor did she tell me anything about you. The message she just sent me stated her apology for making Saul late last night for his shift, but she needed to be sure we met." His gaze turned curious. "You used her too?"

Wyatt nodded and considered this. How could it be possible? And how could Madame Eve know Rye would be so determined to make it happen? As his mind raced, trying to piece it all together, their phones again beeped in unison. Wyatt glanced down toward the lit screen.

Since I suspect you two are probably trying to figure it all out, always remember, I know you better than you know yourselves, and if you recall, the questionnaire stated you wouldn't always know when and how you'd find your match. But I gave my word, I wouldn't disappoint. I suggest you stop staring at each other and simply enjoy the happiness you've discovered.

Madame Eve

Wyatt burst out laughing, Rye followed right behind. "Unfucking-believable." Wyatt had wanted a woman, asked for a woman. How did Madame Eve know him well enough to arrange this? To know that deep down he longed to experience this? If he believed in magic, he might think it held a role there.

The experience far exceeded the expectations he'd placed on Madame Eve when he'd paid for her services in advance. Nothing he could compare it to. No limits. Excessive pleasure.

Continuing to chuckle, Wyatt strode toward his clothes while Rye watched from the bed, nearly undressing the clothes Wyatt put on with his stare.

"Mind not looking at me like that? My cock is already harder than fuck," Wyatt grated.

"I've got no control that my body isn't finished with you." Rye emphasized it by wrapping his hand around his erection and giving it a tug.

Wyatt's gaze trained on the man, which made his blood burn. He murmured erotic whispers, turning away to the mirror and ran a hand through his hair to straighten it then placed the cap on. He dug into his pocket to take out a piece of gum to freshen his mouth. He'd wasted enough time already, he didn't want to worry about his breath now. He needed to get to Katrina. Once settled, he glanced back to Rye who hadn't let up stroking his hard length.

"You plan on coming back after you catch whoever you're after?" Rye's question hung through the air and a little moan escaped his firm lips as his hand slid down to the base of his cock.

Wyatt stepped forward, grabbed the tip of Rye's cock and squeezed hard. Rye wheezed, his eyes shut and he shuddered. Wyatt's own groin awakened with a burning need to indulge himself in Rye's talents, yet he understood his reasons for being there and his obligations to his job.

Keeping his hand on Rye, he leaned forward and kissed Rye's mouth. A reminder for what Wyatt had to offer him. The experience wasn't about a happily ever after nor about two hearts joining, it lingered on pure lust. Two men sharing the same want to fuck until their bodies were exhausted.

Wyatt released his hand, backed away from Rye's mouth and stood, turning on his heel he strode to the door. Opening it wide and not giving a flying fuck who saw, he looked over his shoulder. "Count on it."

SOMEWHERE IN BETWEEN

BY

STACEY KENNEDY

PROLOGUE

Wyatt Tanning stared at the paperwork on his desk. He read over his notes for the hundredth time, clenching his jaw in frustration. Ten days and counting, and the shady criminal who stared back at him from the mug shot remained on the run.

Marcus Walsh had spent the majority of his young adult life in and out of prison. Now, in his late thirties, he'd done unthinkable things to women—ending in murder.

Weeks ago, the police discovered a body, and saliva found on the victim belonged to Marcus. As the Chief Deputy of the U.S. Marshals, Wyatt's ass was on the line when a criminal avoided capture, and the director had been riding him hard lately for his failures on the case. Not a position he enjoyed. If anyone rode his ass, he wanted Rye Daniels to do it.

"Heading home for the night, boss?"

The soft voice startled Wyatt away from his thoughts. He glanced up to find his second in command, Taryn, leaning up against the doorframe. "As soon as we catch Marcus, I will be."

"Tough case, isn't it?"

"That's an understatement." He ran his hands over his face and sighed. Endless clues gave them hope—only to result in disappointment. They were no closer to catching Marcus than when Wyatt picked up the case file, and the worry Marcus had abducted more women sat heavy on his shoulders. "I don't have a clue where to go from here." He lowered his hand and looked at Taryn. "You?"

She shook her head. "Let's call it night and we can start fresh tomorrow. Run through the files again to see if we've missed something. I'm sure Rye's waiting for you to come home, and I know I'm exhausted."

The mention of Wyatt's lover should have worried him, considering only Taryn knew of his same-sex relationship. But no one else in their department remained in the station at the late hour, exactly why she would say the remark so casually. "I'm sure he is and you're right, we're all exhausted. There's no point continuing the search until we get some rest."

He'd been craving Rye, not only because he missed the comfort his lover gave to him, but he needed an outlet from the mounting frustration. Yes, he planned to sleep, but first he'd release the negative energy burning in his blood.

Wyatt closed the file with a slam, and stood to approach Taryn when his phone beeped. "Dammit." He reached into his pocket to view the email message. He stared at the screen disbelieving what he read.

"Who's it from?" The high-pitched squeak in Taryn's tone confirmed the shock in his expression.

He needed to understand the message before he'd say anything to her about its contents. He turned away and returned to his desk. "Give me a minute here."

"Okay," she said warily and left the room.

Her tone held more questions, and he could understand it. But right then, the world spun and he needed to get hold of himself. He sank down into his seat to read the message. He glanced over it once and read it again for good measure, but more slowly.

I'm sending this message to you as I know you've been having trouble on a case you're currently involved in. I cannot speak of my sources, but I can tell you a woman at 114 Campbell Street by the name of Darby Grant needs your help. I hope my contacting you will assist in this matter.

Warmest regards,
Madame Eve

He hadn't been in contact with Madame Eve—the woman who owned the 1Night Stand matchmaking service—for a good two months. He'd originally used her to help find him the woman of his dreams. Instead, he'd been matched with Rye and was thankful she'd known his needs better than he had at the time.

Why had she contacted him now? How was she aware of the case he worked on? Even though he had questions, he wouldn't waste the information. Madame Eve had an uncanny ability to know things others didn't, and a lead was a lead, no matter where it came from.

"Taryn," he called out.

She trotted back into the room. "What's up?" she asked, eagerness in her eyes, even if confusion showed in her expression.

"I've got a lead here." He shook his phone in his hand. "Call the team back in. We've got to go to 114 Campbell Street."

Taryn's brow furrowed. "Where did the lead come from?"

"It's not important." It'd take too long to go through all the details with her, and in truth, he couldn't quite believe it himself. Getting Taryn to understand would waste time—time they didn't have. "Go now."

Without hesitation, Taryn ran from the room, and he heard her calling the other deputies back in. He didn't know if Madame Eve had Marcus' location right, nor did he care. They had exhausted all the leads so far, and he'd take any help offered to find the bastard.

Wyatt drove down Gregg Street in Houston, Texas. The siren atop his truck blared in the night while he pushed the truck far past acceptable speed limits.

Low class, economy houses whipped by the driver's side window, but being close to midnight he wasn't concerned about injuring someone if they stepped out onto the road. Elderly people would be fast asleep and so would children. Anyone up at the late hour knew enough to get out of his way.

He glanced in the rearview mirror and spotted Taryn's truck behind him with the four deputies inside. He focused back on the road, passed Nobel Street and pushed harder on the gas pedal, gripping the steering wheel tight. His urgency wasn't only to catch Marcus. He worried that Marcus held other women there who needed rescuing besides Darby Grant.

As he drove on, a thought rose that he couldn't push away. The last time Madame Eve contacted him had been the night he met Rye. He wondered if somehow she'd set this up for him to find him the match he'd originally asked for—a woman to form a life with.

Rye made him happy, but Wyatt longed for a woman to bear his children. Now though, he asked himself if that could even be possible. He had no intention of ending the relationship with Rye, and he hadn't met any woman who'd want a ménage relationship with two male lovers.

Lee Street passed by in a blur. He shook the thought from his mind. How could Madame Eve have arranged this? There was no way she'd set up such a dangerous situation for Wyatt to meet a woman. He snorted at the absurdity.

He sped toward Campbell Street, grabbed his phone from the dash, and clicked to initiate the radio. "Ya'll ready?"

"Ready and eager, sir," Taryn responded.

He threw the phone onto the seat. The abandoned house came into view. His heart raced. The windows were boarded up, the garden wild, and the grass dead from the hot summer sun. The house barely stood—whitewash peeled off the warped wood, while a porch falling to pieces led to the front door.

At the corner, he slammed on his brakes, threw the truck into park, and cut the engine. Grabbing his flashlight off the passenger seat, he jumped out, ran around the front of the truck, and drew his weapon with his team right on his heels.

He sprinted up the front porch, hearing the wood crack and groan under his weight. At the front door, he raised his foot and kicked it open with a crash. Holding his weapon at shoulder height, he placed the flashlight underneath to offer light in the dark space and entered cautiously.

"Spread out," he ordered.

His team dispersed, each taking a room to search. Wyatt strode forward and kept his gun in his line of vision. He scoped out the living room, if he could even call it such. Old furniture situated around the room sat covered in dust—so much in fact, it itched his nose.

"Clear," Taryn called from the kitchen.

He glanced around, looking behind the couch first then searched every place someone might hide. He found nothing. "Clear," he replied. Each of the deputies issued the same response from upstairs to confirm the house lay empty.

Lowering his gun, he sighed. He'd hoped the lead Madame Eve gave would have brought them to Marcus. Apparently, she'd been wrong, and that not only confused but irritated him. His hopes had risen only to plummet again.

He spun around to approach Taryn in the kitchen, and a light caught his eye. If he'd come in the daytime he never would've seen it, but being pitch black in the room, the light glowed through the dark space. A small hole, maybe the size of a pea, sat at the bottom of the far wall.

Wyatt raised his gun and approached. "I've got something here." At the wall, he squatted and ran his finger over the light. He looked to Taryn when she stepped in next to him. "There's something behind here."

He stood, raised his leg, and after a few well-placed kicks, his foot went through the wall. He peered through the hole to see a set of stairs, and a wall lined with soundproofing. Turning his gun around, he used the butt end to bash through.

The loud cracking of wood filled his ears, but the second he stopped, something else registered in the air—a loud scream for help. He jerked his head toward Taryn. "Did you hear that?"

"I heard it." She pushed on his back. "Go."

He squeezed through the hole and ran down the stairs, searching for the location of the scream. Taryn, joined by the other deputies, stayed right on his heels.

After hitting the last step, he kept his gun and flashlight up, and scanned the area. The basement consisted of stone walls. To the left was a hallway he could only assume had been recently added, since it didn't appear to have been built with the original house, and more so, had been dug out. He had no idea what they were walking into and glanced at Taryn, raising his finger to his lips as a precaution.

They silently proceeded down the hallway. There were five doors with no windows or anything else to indicate what stood behind them, but the scream for help came again. His heart skipped a beat and reality set in.

"We'll come back for them," he whispered over his shoulder at Taryn. They needed to press on to see if Marcus stayed there. Undoubtedly, they'd discovered where he housed the women he'd abducted.

The cries of women sounded all around him. He'd never been so disgusted in his life. Clearly, they'd been caged like animals underground, and although the trauma on the body from Marcus' last victim showed he hadn't raped her, it appeared he had tortured her.

The hallway ended at a door with a dead bolt. He kept his weapon up, but with his free hand he reached for the lock. He drew in a deep breath, attempted to open it, but it didn't budge. Stepping back, he kicked the door and it sprang open.

Rushing into the room, he was unable to process the scene in front of him. Against the back wall, strung up against steel bars, a woman hung by her wrists with her head bowed. If that wasn't enough to horrify him, her naked body was marked with what looked like welts from a whip.

He scanned the small, dungeon-like room. There was nowhere to hide—only bare walls and a dirt floor. Clearly, Marcus had already left. He lowered his weapon and hurried over to the woman bound to the bars.

Placing his fingers on the side of her neck, he searched for a pulse, relieved to find it strong and steady. He hooked his finger under her chin to draw her face up. Covered with dirt and grime, she didn't rouse, her long, brown hair knotted and straggly. His heart bled for her.

"Go check those rooms for other victims," he said to the deputies. "Get the paramedics and the crime scene folks here, and bring me a blanket when they come."

The others left the room in rush. Wyatt grabbed the rope on the woman's right wrist and removed it, grimacing at the deep burns along her skin. He made quick work of the other. She slid along her back and sank down, and he let her, not wanting to touch her. She had so many injuries, he didn't want to cause her more pain.

But what choice do I have? He had to get her out of there. Reaching down, he hooked his arms under her legs and back. The moment he stood, the woman's eyes opened, and she screamed.

The sound would haunt him until the day he died.

Even though pain laced Darby's body, her wrists didn't bear the weight of her body any longer, and that freedom offered her a means to get away. But the second she struggled, warm arms tightened around her. "Please don't fight. You're going to hurt yourself further. I'm a U.S. Marshal. You're safe."

She forced her eyes open. Her vision finally focused and warm chocolate eyes stared back at her. The stranger holding her wore a U.S. Marshal's baseball cap, and a bulletproof vest, giving strength to his words. "I'm safe?"

He nodded. "I'm U.S. Marshal Wyatt Tanning, and you are...?"

Her voice sounded scratchy through her dry throat. "Darby Grant."

"How are you feeling, Darby?"

Her whole body hurt, her head ached, and the muggy air coated her naked skin. Yet the reality that she was safe made all of it unimportant. "I'm still alive." She covered her breasts with her arms, yet couldn't find much more strength than that to care that she was nude in a stranger's arms. His appearance meant protection. She didn't want him to let her go. "How did you find us?"

"We've been on this case for some time. A lead brought us to this location." He studied her. "I can answer any questions you need later, but right now, there are more important matters. Do you have any family I should contact?"

She shook her head. "Not here. They're all back in Alabama."

"I can call them—"

"No!" Her exclamation caused his eyes to widen. She inhaled and reined in her outburst. "I don't want them to know what happened to me." She had lived on her own since the age of eighteen. She hadn't needed them then, and now at twenty-seven, she certainly didn't want to contact them.

"Won't they be worried about you? I'm sure they've realized you went missing."

Tears filled her eyes, but she blinked them away, forcing herself to stay strong. "No, I only call home once a month."

He frowned. "But they should know what happened to you."

"No, please, there's no reason to tell them this—they'd overreact and besides, we're not close." Not that she disliked her parents, but Mary Jo and Scott Grant never should have had offspring. They were twenty-year-olds living in sixty-year-old bodies. She'd never been a priority and their relationship was distant. Holidays, special occasions, and monthly phone calls were all they'd needed to call themselves good parents.

The Marshal gave her a puzzled look before he sighed. "All right, it's your choice if you don't want to contact them. However, we should get you to the hospital to clean up your injuries."

Hospital? Oh no. She'd see people she worked with, when all she wanted to do—had wanted to do since the night that changed her life forever—was go home. "I'm a nurse. My injuries are superficial and I can tend to them myself. I want to go home."

His eyebrow lifted. "The welts along your body will be painful to clean up yourself. Besides, you'll be safer there. Marcus Walsh has yet to be captured."

She hadn't even had time to consider if they'd caught Marcus or if he evaded the Marshals. Truth was, she didn't care. All that mattered was he no longer held her prisoner. The hell was over. And she'd survived.

"I want to go home," she repeated. She'd been strong since she turned eight years old and realized her parents didn't intend to care for her. She needed no one, and she liked it that way. She wanted to crawl into her bed and try to find a way back from the past days and nights of terror.

Wyatt paused, considering her as if he had a thousand questions on his mind. Finally, his eyebrows furrowed and intensity burned in the depths of his eyes. "You're going to the hospital. This isn't negotiable. When you're ready, I need to get a report from you, but that can wait until the morning after you've been taken care of."

All she wanted was her house, her place of sanctuary, but by the firm set of his lips, she wasn't going to get what she wanted. "Okay. But then in the morning I can go home, right?"

"Of course." He inclined his head. "I'm going to set you down now."

She bit her lip and prepared herself for the pain. The moment her bottom hit the ground, her injuries protested and she groaned. Marcus had whipped her in what he had called *submissive training*. Darby knew of BDSM. What he had done was nothing like the consensual acts she understood existed in the lifestyle. Purely sadistic, the psychopath tried to get her to submit to him, but she'd rather have died. If the Marshals hadn't come, she suspected she wouldn't have lasted another day.

"I'm sorry, I know that hurts," Wyatt whispered. He slid his arms out from beneath her knees and neck, but remained kneeling beside her.

A female Marshal entered through the hallway with a blanket in her hands. She smiled at Darby, but it looked forced. "Here, sweetie, let me put this over you." She draped it around Darby's shoulders.

Seconds later, the paramedics entered the room.

Darby clutched the blanket and stared at the walls that had caged her. Walls she thought were going to be her grave. The ordeal might have been over, but she doubted she'd ever be the same person again.

How could she go on from there?

Chapter One

One month later....

Darby mourned the woman she once was. Why did she have to go out *that* night after her shift at the hospital to start her week of vacation? Why did she have to talk with *him*—tell him her whole life story and spell out no one would know she was gone? And why had she taken the drink Marcus had offered her, which she assumed he'd laced with Rohypnol?

If she hadn't gone out for a night of fun alone, the event that forever changed her life a month ago wouldn't have happened. But her therapist suggested she needed to get out and face the world again. Hiding in her home would get her nowhere.

She kept her groceries tight in her hand and walked down the street as dusk settled in around her.

How did this happen? She once had a life, maybe not a perfect one, but one she'd been proud of. Every day did get easier, yet she doubted she'd ever find peace. How could she drink a coffee at Starbucks? Go back to the hospital and see injuries on others, and not be reminded of what had happened to her?

It had taken the past four weeks for the marks on her body to fade. But while the outside no longer showed the evidence of her horrific few days—the inside of her would never heal. How could she recover? Tears formed in her eyes. Things would never be the same again. She had no idea how to put one foot in front of the other. But she'd follow her therapist's advice: one step at a time.

She inhaled deeply, smelling exhaust and fast food. Rounding the corner onto Haver Street, she eyed her traditional, one-story home. She'd painted the outside yellow a month before the abduction. With the tulip garden leading the way to the front door, the house always charmed her. The tightness in her chest eased, and she approached the cherry red front door painted to match the flowers.

Home.

She shifted the grocery bags into one hand, trotted up the front steps, and reached for the door. Her hand froze mid-way. The door was open a crack. Panic sent a wave of heat washing through her, rendering her incapable of moving. Her lips parted to release the scream in her throat, but her fear left her motionless.

As far as she knew, Marcus remained on the run and the thought had crossed her mind, every second of the day, that he'd come after her. But she always settled her worry with the knowledge that he didn't know where she lived. Could he have found her?

She scanned the area. The night seemed darker now. Shadows crept around her. She trembled and frightened tears dampened her cheeks.

"Darby."

She startled, dropping her grocery bags to the floor. She

spun around in horror of what she'd face. But the moment her eyes landed on the man behind her, she released the breath she held. "Oh, God."

Wyatt—the Marshal she'd met in the dungeon—approached her. "I'm here to help." He stopped and raised his hands. "Just breathe. You're okay."

Tears flowed heavily down her cheeks. She shook her head and her heart raced.

"Come with me." He stepped forward.

She receded backward. "No. What's going on here? Why is my door open?"

"Shhh...I know you're afraid, but I want to get you out of here."

She stared into his eyes, but her fear caused her to distrust him. "I don't understand what's going on."

He took another step toward her. "Your house was broken into tonight."

Her pounding heart forced sweat to form over her skin. The world spun. "How do you know that?"

He settled in front of her. His height made her angle her head back and his thick build unsettled her. "I've been keeping an eye on you for the last month."

She gulped. "Why?"

"We haven't caught Marcus yet, and I suspected he might return for you." His face twisted with emotion. "I didn't want to leave you alone."

None of what he said made any sense. She had no idea why he was protecting her or why she hadn't been told about it. She needed answers. "Why?"

He paused, studying her then finally said, "It's important you come with me and we get you to a safe location. While driving over here to watch the house for the night, I was notified that something triggered your security alarm. I'm sorry, but I did go into your house and look around, although the intruder had already left by the time I got here. I suspect the alarm scared him away."

She wobbled on her feet. "I-I-I...need to sit down for minute." Bile rose in her throat.

Wyatt grabbed her arm and she didn't have the strength to pull away. His touch comforted her regardless that she thought any touch again would frighten her. He assisted her to sit on the front step. "Put your head between your knees. Just breathe."

Darby inhaled, deeply. The world did summersaults around her. She tried to fight off the wicked memories of her time in the basement, but each one came rushing back into her mind, making her stomach clench. She placed her hand over her mouth, gagged, and ran over to the bushes to vomit.

Many minutes passed before the gripping panic settled and her stomach emptied. She wiped her mouth, sitting back on her legs. She dropped her face into her hands and sobbed. For what happened. For what could have happened if she'd returned and Marcus had been there. And mostly for the reality she couldn't get away from.

The nightmare of her life.

Wyatt's tone sounded tight behind her. "Please tell me what I can do for you."

She glanced over her shoulder to find him with fists clenched. His intense reaction stole the lingering fear. His concern seemed genuine. "I'm feeling better now." She forced the images from her mind to gather strength. Now that the fear had fled, the daunting situation made it clear she wasn't safe there. But one problem presented itself. "I have nowhere else to go."

"I can set you up in a hotel until this is over."

That sounded good and all. It wasn't like she needed to stay at her house, since she wasn't working, but he hadn't considered something. "How much safer am I there? He found me here."

"I'll get the room next to you until this is over."

Relief soared through her. But why would he offer such a thing? "Is that not putting you out at all?"

He shook his head. "I'll stay there at night and when I need to work during the day, I'll have a patrol officer stay with you."

Why is he going out of his way for me? "Are the other victims under this sort of protection?"

"They're all with family members, but since you don't have that option, we need to offer you another means of safety. Come on, I'll take you inside so you can gather your things."

She'd never burden her family with this mess. Her fear assured her that she couldn't face her attacker if he returned. She'd been defenseless. She wasn't about to refuse the Marshal's kind offer. "Okay, let's go."

Whatever happened from there, at least she was safe.

She hoped.

CHAPTER TWO

Wyatt had never offered such a thing before, but he didn't want to leave her in danger. He could have stationed at patrol officer by her door. However, he wanted to look out for her, just as he had been for the last month.

No one asked him to take on the task, but he couldn't get Darby off his mind. He couldn't explain the need to ensure what happened to her before didn't happen again. Seeing Marcus had returned for her, he was glad he'd kept tabs on her.

He turned his truck onto John Kennedy Boulevard and the Clarion appeared halfway down the road. The large hotel by the airport was a good choice. Not that it mattered much; he'd pay for this out of his own pocket. He'd not dare put the expense through the department and have the director asking questions.

Pulling into a parking spot, he cut the engine. He grabbed Darby's luggage from the bed of the truck and met her on the other side. She followed and he entered the hotel. "Just take a seat here and I'll get everything settled."

She sat down in a chair in the lobby and he proceeded to the concierge desk. After a quick exchange, he paid for the hotel rooms for a week then reached into his pocket and pulled out his cell phone.

Rye's phone went straight to voicemail. He left a quick message to meet him there with clothes for the next week.

He returned to find Darby fidgeting with her fingers. "I got us adjoining rooms. I hope you're all right with that."

She nodded and stood. "I don't mind if it means I'm safe."

He smiled, pleased she was being so willing. The situation bothered him much more than it should. He'd been around many victims before and he'd never taken such a personal interest in one. Why he wanted to ensure her safety was unclear, but he'd learned not to ignore his instincts. And they told him to watch out for her. He had no intention of doing otherwise.

"Let's get you comfortable then." He strode forward, and she followed behind. At Room 101, he slid the card into the reader and entered the room. The space was exactly what he expected to find—typical, plain hotel room. But it'd suffice.

He placed her bags on the dresser and turned back to her. She sat on the bed, her head bowed, and she clenched her hands together on her lap. "I can't believe this is happening."

His heart ached for her. He knelt down in front of her, took her chin, and angled her head up. "We'll find him. I promise. This is just a safety precaution."

"I actually was just settling into things again." She shrugged with a sigh. "I mean, at least, venturing out of the house and acknowledging life. Why would he come back for me?"

"Psychopaths like him have no rhyme or reason for the things they do. If I went on my hunch, I'd say it's because he thinks you belong to him and he wants you back." The evidence he'd gathered not only from a psychologist, but Darby's statement and the other women as well, led him to believe

Marcus Walsh acted on Master/slave behavior.

A tear slid down her cheek. "I'm just so tired of all this. I want to have my normal life back."

He wanted nothing more than to wipe the tear away, but he refrained. He had to wonder if what she wanted was possible. Could anyone recover from what she'd been through? Could she pick up the pieces of her broken life and find her way? He had no answers for that.

"Once we capture him—and we will—your life will settle and you'll find the peace you deserve."

Tears flowed down her cheeks. "I hope so."

He stayed quiet, studying her. *What is it about this woman that brings out these protective feelings in me?* Why did he feel if he saved her, he'd be saving himself, too? His mind swept away with thoughts, a knock at the door jolted him back to the present.

Her eyes widened and she tensed. "Who's here?"

He stood. "I called a friend of mine to come and bring me some clothes." He strode toward the door. As he opened it, he was sideswiped and slammed against the wall.

"You know, if I knew moving to Houston to be with you would mean I only see you a minute out of each day, I might have reconsidered." Rye dropped to his knees and raised his hands to unbuckle Wyatt's belt, grinning to show he said his statement in jest.

Wyatt grabbed Rye's hand. "Not a good time." He gestured toward Darby, who sat with her mouth hanging open.

"Oh." Rye laughed, dropping his hands. He stood and gave the grin that could harden Wyatt's groin if he let it. He saw by the flicker of ease in Darby's expression that it worked its charm on her, too. He glanced back at Wyatt. "When you called me, I thought you were in the middle of a case and got to take a break."

Darby inhaled deeply and stood straight up in flash. "Er...um...I'm sorry to have interrupted...."

"No apologies necessary," Rye replied. "I hadn't known Wyatt was staying here with a guest."

She twisted her hands nervously. "Well, you see, I'm not really a guest."

Wyatt watched her struggle for words and stepped in before she was placed in another awkward situation. "Rye, this is Darby. Darby, meet Rye Daniels. Darby was involved in the Marcus Walsh case. He broke into her house tonight. So, I've decided to bring her here as a precaution." Rye's eyes widened and clear questions burned in their depths, but Wyatt would fill him in later. Darby was the priority. "Did you bring my clothes?"

Rye scooted back out into the hall and returned with two bags in his hands. "Brought my stuff, too—figured this was the only way I'd see you."

Wyatt glanced back to Darby to find her staring at them curiously. He hoped their relationship didn't make her feel uncomfortable. "Would it be better for you if he didn't stay?"

She looked at Rye then back at Wyatt before she shrugged. "In all honesty, having both of you around just makes me feel safer. Then if Marcus comes here, he'll be outnumbered. So no, I don't mind."

Rye grinned. "Wyatt's got a gun and I'm a fighter with the Ultimate Fighting Championship. The fucker wouldn't get a foot inside of this hotel room—that I can promise you."

She smiled, even though it appeared forced. "Thank you."

"Will you be all right in here or do you want us to stay with you until you've fallen asleep?" Wyatt asked.

"I'll be okay." She approached her bags and removed some pajamas. "I'm just going to have a bath, and crawl into bed."

"Don't expect to sleep much. Wyatt snores like a freight train." Rye chuckled.

Wyatt socked him. "I do not."

Darby laughed and the sweet sound sent a warm wave of emotion washing over Wyatt. It was the first time he'd ever heard her laugh. For the past month, all he'd seen was sadness when she walked along the street or when he spied her through her window, sitting on her plush couch and reading a book. Her posture rose and her chin lifted. He couldn't help but smile in return.

"We'll let Darby be the judge of that tomorrow after we wake up." Rye continued chuckling as he left the room.

Wyatt followed, but when he reached the adjoining door, he glanced over his shoulder. "I'll close this for now to give you some privacy. If it's all right, I'd like to open it later to make sure I'm aware if anything were to happen."

She nodded without hesitation. "I'm okay with that."

"Sleep well." He watched her head off to the bathroom. He closed the adjoining hotel door behind him and turned around to see Rye taking a seat on the bed, staring at him with amusement dancing in his eyes.

"What's with the look?" Wyatt asked.

Rye smiled. "I see now why you've been so insistent on watching over her. She's quite beautiful."

Wyatt would be blind if he didn't notice the stunning Darby. The woman had captured his mind the last month. But those thoughts weren't important now. "She's been through hell."

Rye arched an eyebrow. "I never said anything about what she's been through, or what she's thinking, merely that she's something sweet to look at." A challenge rose in the depths of his blue eyes. "A bit defensive, aren't we?"

Wyatt snorted. "No."

"Oh, really." Rye gave the classic Rye expression, full of arrogance. "You telling me you're not trying to come up with reasons not to find her attractive?"

Had he been doing that? He hadn't thought so, but maybe Rye was onto something. Wyatt pondered only a moment before he scowled, pissed that Rye might have been right, but hell bent to prove him wrong. "You have no idea what you're talking about."

"Aw, it's sweet satisfaction proving you're full of shit." Rye snickered.

Wyatt strode toward the dresser to take off his watch. Desperate to change the subject, he focused on something he had yet to share with Rye. He'd held back because he still hadn't sorted it all out himself. Plus he'd hardly seen Rye. "I've been holding off on telling you something, since there's been a lot going on with this case. But something happened that I think you might take an interest in." He pulled his T-shirt off, folded it, and placed it on the dresser.

"I can't imagine anything you experienced on this case I'd take an interest in," Rye said with a bite to each word.

Wyatt dropped his jeans, set them with the shirt, and turned back to find Rye's clothes in a heap on the floor. Not a surprise—his neatness left something to be desired. "I got an email from Madame Eve about this case."

Rye's eyebrows furrowed. "What did she say?"

"She was the lead that gave up the location to find Darby and the other women. Fuck me, she was right." He removed his socks. "I have no idea how she would have known about this."

"Well, she's proven herself to know things others don't," Rye offered.

"That's true." He shrugged. "I have no doubt her involvement is an innocent one, but I plan to find out how she knew what she did once I have a chance to breathe." He sat next to Rye. "Nevertheless, I'm only glad she had the information. That fucker had himself quite a set up, and those women wouldn't have survived much longer in those conditions."

Rye frowned. "Damn, Wyatt, I don't know how you do this fucking job." He placed his hand on Wyatt's shoulder, squeezing firmly. "Are you doing all right?"

Wyatt hadn't even thought of himself yet, and he'd be lying if he said the whole experience hadn't affected him. He gave Rye the honest answer he searched for. "This month has been draining. It's dead end after dead end. And with doing the surveillance on her house, I've slept a total of two hours a night."

He ran his hands over his face. Heaviness weighed on his shoulders. He lowered his hands, not bothering to look at Rye. "I'm going to shower." He pushed off the bed and strode into the bathroom.

At the shower, he turned the water on hot. The second he stepped under the spray, he sighed and placed his hands against the tile to let the water drip down his head and along his back.

Mere minutes passed before a hard body pressed against his. Rye's erect cock settled against the seam of his ass. Fuck, it felt good. After the strain of everything, after not seeing Rye or being intimate with him for over a month, he craved the man.

Rye slid his hand over Wyatt's hip and grabbed onto his semi-erect dick. He stroked it while rubbing his own erection against Wyatt's ass. Wyatt leaned his head back to send the water splashing against his chest and drew in a deep breath.

"I've been wanting this for a month now," Rye whispered huskily in Wyatt's ear. "I know where your priorities lie, but damn, I've missed you."

Wyatt spun around and the water sprayed his back. Rye kept a tight hold on his erection. "Best I don't keep you waiting then."

Wyatt pushed on Rye's shoulders in a demand his lover give him the pleasure he sought.

Rye didn't deny his request. He sank to his knees and took Wyatt deep into his throat. Wyatt groaned. His muscles tensed. Nothing compared to Rye's mouth around his cock—the man could suck him so good it made him cross-eyed.

He offered languorous sucks, licked his shaft, along his balls, and never let up for a moment. Wyatt clenched his fists at his sides, staring down. Rye ran his lips over his shaft, before issuing another round of purposeful flicks of his tongue to drive Wyatt to near insanity.

Wyatt moaned, closed his eyes, and leaned his head back to let the water run along his face, down his chest and drip onto his hard on. Rye backed away, gripped Wyatt's erection and jerked him off—hard, tight, fast strokes, causing him to thrust along with each movement.

His balls drew up. His need to come enveloped him, but he wanted Rye to come with him. He latched onto his arm and pulled him up. "Come here."

Rye grinned, stood and pressed himself against Wyatt's dick. Wyatt leaned forward and kissed him with all the intensity burning in his veins. Lips crushed against each other in a fevered pitch. He latched onto Rye's cock and stroked it with the same rhythm Rye set. He squeezed Rye until he reached the tip, where he swirled his hand and teased the head.

Rye grunted. He deepened the kiss. Tongues clashed together. Deep moans filled the shower. Wyatt took a step back to allow the water to touch Rye's body and offer him the same warm embrace.

Then he picked up speed—encased Rye's cock in his hand and pumped, hard and fast. He grabbed his neck and held him firm, a tight hold to ensure neither of them moved while they fist-fucked each other.

Rye's movements mirrored Wyatt's, and several strokes later, Wyatt's stomach clenched. He backed away, kept the hold on his lover's neck, and held eye contact with him. Rye's gaze burned molten and his jaw clenched. Wyatt grunted, a sound Rye echoed.

With a shudder, Wyatt released all his tension and bathed Rye's hand with his cum, while Rye followed right along.

After a few deep breaths to regain himself, he leaned his forehead against Rye's. "I've missed you, too."

Rye chuckled. "Clearly."

CHAPTER THREE

Sweat soaked Darby's body. Her legs trembled. The whip burned against her skin. She stared out at the underground room and pain soared through her. The rope binding her wrists was looped through rings on the steel wall. Her back pressed tight against the cold metal.

How much more could she take? "I'm sorry, Master." She hoped her last apology would appease the man before her.

His dark, cruel eyes stared at her—a vicious glare that would haunt her forever. "I don't believe you." When he whipped her again, Darby's muscles tensed. "We've had three days together now, Darby, and your progress is nothing to marvel over." Again, he twisted his wrist to snap the whip along her torso.

She cringed.

Nights of submissive training—as he called it—left her exhausted. "I'm not sure what you want of me, Master." If only he'd tell her, explicitly, she'd respond to his demands. Maybe then he'd stop hurting her.

The man paced in front of her like an animal intent on a kill. He towered over her, his dark hair dangling over his forehead—everything about him screamed danger, and Darby had no one to protect her.

"I want you to submit," he snarled before whipping her.

Again....

And again....

Darby shot straight up in bed, hugging herself. It'd only been a nightmare...a reenactment of the past. She scanned the room, instantly reminded she wasn't in that basement anymore, but horror shook her soul. She panted, attempting to get air into her lungs. Her tight throat made her breathing labored. The fear of being alone left her incapacitated—she parted her lips to call out for Wyatt, desperately needing to be with someone, yet nothing came out.

Drenched with sweat, panic filled her. The darkness of the room created shadows making her quake in fright. She couldn't be alone.

The shadows closed in on her and she needed comfort. She forced her feet to work, slid out of bed, and crossed the room. Stepping through the door to the other room, she found both Wyatt and Rye in the bed, and their deep breaths sounded soft while they slept.

"Wyatt," she whispered.

She stepped forward. Her eyes adjusted to the lack of light. Wyatt slept on his side on the left, angled away from Rye, who slept on his back. She hated to wake them, but had no other choice. She cleared her throat. "Wyatt."

Wyatt startled and jumped out of bed. "What's wrong?"

"I'm...I-I-I...."

He approached her, his expression fixed with worry. "Are you okay? What's happened?"

"What's going on?" Rye murmured, sitting up in bed.

"I had a nightmare, and I'm...." She had no idea how to voice her thoughts to strangers. *I'm so afraid and I can't be alone.*

Wyatt studied her for a moment before he gave his head a good shake, clearly to wake up. Finally, after a long pause, he said, "Did something scare you?"

Tears welled in her eyes. She nodded.

Rye turned on the night table light. He squinted, examining her, and said, "Do you not want to be alone?"

The tears spilled down her cheeks. She shook her head.

Rye snuck out of bed, wearing only briefs and she noticed a dragon tattoo along his chest that ran over his shoulder. He held the covers open for her. "You can stay here in the bed, and we'll take to the floor."

She shook her head again.

Both Wyatt and Rye stared blank-faced at her.

As odd as it all was, she needed someone—and something—that made her feel safe in the scary reality of her life. She needed it so desperately she found her voice. "Can I stay with you?"

Wyatt's eyes widened. "In the bed?"

"Please. I know it's strange, but I need to be close to someone right now." Her voice trembled. "I'm so afraid."

Both men said nothing, staring at her intently. Finally, Rye returned to the bed. "Come on then, crawl in."

Wyatt jerked his head toward him. "Rye!"

"What?" Rye frowned. "She wouldn't be asking if she didn't really need it. Think about it, Wyatt." He shifted on his side of the bed and patted the space beside him. "Time's a wastin' and I'm tired. Get on in, Darby. You'll be safe here."

She hesitated, knowing Wyatt wasn't on board with the offer. But in truth, she couldn't pass up the invitation. There was no way she could go back to her room to be alone, and furthermore, she craved something she'd missed this past month—the reminder of being embraced.

She approached the bed and Rye held the sheets up for her to squirm in. Once she'd settled in the middle, she lay on her back and held the blankets up to her chin. Weird as it may be, since the first time the whole nightmare began, she felt eased.

Rye rolled over and turned off the light. "I'm going to sleep now, and I don't know about you, but standing while trying to sleep might prove to be difficult." When the light flicked off, he pulled the blanket up under his armpits and snuggled into his pillow.

Wyatt stood on the other side of the room for a moment before returning to the bed, and settled in on the other side of Darby. Rye squirmed closer toward her and Wyatt did as well, but neither of the men touched her.

Darby sighed, the fear and panic slowly easing, replaced by something else entirely that shocked her. She wanted them to touch her. Was she reacting to the fear she'd experienced and emotionally out of control? *Is that why I'm feeling this way?*

Whatever the reason, she tried to shove the reaction away, but it was pointless. All she could think of were the two warm-bodied, strong men who lay beside her.

Chapter Four

The early morning sun shone through the blinds. Wyatt's eyes opened and landed on Darby as she slept on her side. He sighed, watching her. At first, he might have been against the idea of her joining them because it felt entirely wrong. But nothing had ever seemed so right. His reactions to her were more than just saving Darby from the horror thrust upon her. There was something more to *her*. A connection Wyatt hadn't expected to find, nor would he let go of now. He wanted to protect her, hold her there between him and Rye, and keep her safe forever.

Insane.

He closed his eyes, willing himself to stop thinking such things, and listened to the deep breathing around him. He wondered, though, why he had awakened. A moment later, a beep on his phone alerted him to the reason.

He groaned, a sound mirrored by Rye, and rolled over to snatch up his phone on the end table. He clicked the unlock button, and his heart leapt into his throat when he saw the message.

We've got him, boss! We're at headquarters. I'm waiting for you here.

Taryn

He lowered the phone to find Rye had one eye open and stared at him. "They've got him," he whispered.

Both Rye's eyes opened. "Should we wake her?" His voice was equally as quiet—a tone Wyatt hadn't heard come from Rye's normally commanding voice.

Wyatt smiled. Darby made Rye soft sigh. "Nah, go back to sleep. She needs the rest and I don't want to disturb her. I'll deal with this and return shortly." He slid out of bed and went to the bathroom, before he grabbed clothes from the dresser.

Once dressed, he turned back to see Rye on his side and nestled into Darby's back. The happiness that rushed through his soul stole his breath. He knew nothing of Darby, except from the little time he'd been with her. Yet with Rye nuzzled into her, nothing seemed more perfect, and the realization dawned on him.

Madame Eve.

The email she sent rushed back into his thoughts; it'd been her who'd given up Marcus' location. He now suspected his earlier thoughts were correct—she had some part in all this.

He couldn't deny that he felt an instant connection to her, no matter how bizarre the circumstances were. He'd never felt so protective over anyone in his life. He hadn't let her out of his sight for a month now. And when he discovered Marcus had broken into her home, he wanted to kill the man with his bare hands.

But how could Madame Eve have pulled this off? None of it made any sense. Right now, his only thoughts rested on seeing

Marcus behind bars. After a final look at Rye and Darby, he turned on his heels to return to Police Headquarters. He hurried out of the hotel, jumped in his truck, and sped away.

The streets of Houston were quiet in the early morning hour. The light traffic meant a quick drive. He arrived at the station in under ten minutes, parked his truck, and when he opened the door, Taryn's voice greeted him.

"Good, you got here fast."

He approached her. "Tell me what happened?"

She opened the door to the station. "After you informed me of the break-in, I contacted his family and pushed them, hard. I made it quite clear if anyone else died, those lives would rest on their shoulders." She stepped into the station. "His father finally broke and told me the address he stayed at, and also said Marcus hadn't been well for many years."

Wyatt followed her in. Marcus's family had been protective over him and never once offered information on his whereabouts. His fist tightened at the stupidity of their actions. "What do you mean by not well?"

She stopped midway down the hall, and glanced at him. "Mentally ill. No surprise, right?"

Anyone capable of what Marcus had done had to be insane. "Yes, not something I didn't already suspect."

"After we gathered Intel on him, we located his house and did surveillance for an hour or so. Then we breached the home."

"Did he give you any trouble?"

She shook her head. "He'd been sleeping and we acted quickly."

"Well done." He patted her shoulder and her eyes warmed with pride. Her perseverance had paid off. Exactly why they worked opposite shifts—it kept the heat on 24/7. "Has he confessed?"

"He held nothing back, and I mean nothing. He's proud of what he's done."

Disgusting, but again, Wyatt wasn't surprised. He'd suspected Marcus would be satisfied with his accomplishments. He exhaled heavily. "Let's go speak to him, shall we?"

She nodded, opening the door to the interrogation room, and entered. Wyatt followed, and when she moved aside, Marcus appeared, casually leaning against the back wall. Wyatt snorted at the arrogance of the man before him.

"Another pig," Marcus sneered. "What do you want now?"

Wyatt's jaw clenched. Anger bubbled up in his chest. "I want nothing from you. I merely wanted to let my thoughts be known."

Amusement danced in Marcus's dark eyes. "Which are?"

Either the enjoyment Marcus got out of his question or the acknowledgment that there stood the man who dared to abduct Darby, threw him over the edge. Wyatt lurched forward and came face-to-face with her attacker.

"If I could chain you up and deliver the pain you gave not only to Darby, but to all the women you've hurt, I would."

Marcus grinned, cruelly. "Ahh, Darby. She was so luscious."

Anger roared in Wyatt's soul. Without a second thought, or even the concern of his role as a U.S. Marshal, he slugged Marcus across the jaw, sending the man crumbling to the ground. He raised his eyes to Taryn, who smiled at him. Wyatt returned the grin. "Fuck, that felt good."

She inclined her head, laughing. "I'm sure it did, but I can't believe you just decked a suspect. Quite unlike you." She studied him a moment before gesturing to the groaning Marcus. "Best you go now. This alone will have some explaining to do. If he regains his ability to speak again, you're likely do worse to him. I've got it covered. I'll do up the paperwork before I head home."

Wyatt stretched out his hand, exhaling deeply. He'd never let his emotions take hold of him in such a way before, but it only confirmed his suspicions. What he felt toward Darby, no matter how short a time they'd known each other, rang true.

With a nod at Taryn, he left the room, determined to return to Darby to tell her the news.

CHAPTER FIVE

Darby woke surrounded by the warm skin of Rye. His face turned slightly toward her, and his lips were pouty. She couldn't withhold her smile. From what she'd seen of him, he appeared tough, and seeing him like this made him look sweet.

He inhaled deeply and peeked open an eye. "You're brave to get that close to my breath in the mornin'."

After what she'd been through, such meaningless things didn't matter. "You smell just fine." She laughed. It'd felt like forever since she smiled, or even had the energy to laugh. But Rye made things lighter.

He stretched, groaning. "Did you sleep well?"

"I did. I think that was the best sleep I've had in a while. I normally wake up a couple times with nightmares. But once I crawled in here, I slept like a baby."

Both of his eyes opened. He studied her and finally said, "Wyatt told me the extent of what happened to you. I'm sorry."

"It's not you that has anything to be sorry for," she whispered. "I'm not even sure I've accepted it all yet. It's kinda unbelievable, you know?"

"I'd imagine it would be." His gaze shifted to her hand tucked under her cheek before he looked back at her. "May I hold your hand?"

"Why?"

He shrugged. "It feels right to do so."

Strange, but she wanted the same thing. There was a sense of warmth she experienced being with Rye, as well as with Wyatt. She reached out to him, and Rye scooped up her hand and held it against the pillow.

"I really appreciate how great you both are being about this," she said.

His brow furrowed. "You're not putting us out any. Trust me, having a woman in my bed isn't exactly what I'd call a bad way to spend a night."

She laughed. "When you say it like that, it doesn't sound too bad." At first, she'd thought the men were gay, but his admission suggested they were bisexual. Why did that knowledge send a funny feeling rushing through her belly?

Rye's serious expression remained. "If you don't mind me asking, how are you holding up?"

"At first, it was hard to return to everyday life. I mean, it seemed so strange to do normal things, but the counseling really helped and lately, I've ventured out more. I've tried to always tell myself that I wouldn't let him beat me. And I'm still alive. Many of his victims are not. Now, I'm just trying to find my way again. That's the hard part."

His eyes bored intently into hers. "You're a strong woman."

"I've had to be." She sighed at the truth behind her words. "My whole life has been a struggle."

A protective note flashed across his face. "If I could cut the man's balls off and make him eat them, I would."

"And I'd let you, too."

He grinned, the serious expression relaxing. "Wyatt told me last night that you're a nurse. Have you returned to work?"

She shook her head. "I can't go back there. How can I help other people with their injuries when it'll just be a constant reminder of what happened?"

He examined her again. "We'll have to find you something else to do. The good thing about life is you have choices. You just have to discover something that makes you happy and go with it."

Her heart pitter-patted at the way he made her feel like she wasn't alone. "Yes, well, that's what I was trying to do before last night and the horror of all this returned."

His eyes lit up, almost as if he knew something she didn't. He squeezed her hand. "You'll get your life back because you deserve to."

Surprisingly enough, his touch didn't make her flinch. She'd seen cruel eyes, the evil that was present in someone, but none of that existed there. Rye comforted her. "I keep telling myself that and trying to take one step at a time."

He nodded. "That's all you can do."

Being there, close to him, a certain peace settled over her that made her wonder if she'd already found what she was looking for. Suddenly, though, she realized someone was missing. "Where's Wyatt?

"I'm here."

She raised her head to see him leaning against the doorframe with a grin on his face. A smile she couldn't quite place. Yes, he appeared happy, but something more existed in the depths of his eyes. "Where'd you go? And *what* happened to your fingers?"

Wyatt glanced at his battered hand before he waved away

her concern. "It's nothing. I've just returned from the station."

"Clearly, all went well, judging by the swelling on your knuckles?" Rye's voice sounded full of excitement, which led Darby again to believe he knew something she didn't.

Feeling slightly annoyed to be out of the loop, she interjected before Wyatt could respond. "Are you two going to share with me why you both look ready to burst out of your skin?"

Wyatt approached to sit next to her on the bed. "Marcus Walsh was put under arrest this morning."

So many emotions rushed through her; she barely made sense out of them all. Elation, relief, but one stood out among the rest—sadness. As much as she wanted this to be over, she knew it meant she'd have to go home. She liked being there with the two men. She hadn't ever felt so safe, and she didn't want that to end. But Wyatt and Rye had no obligation to her. Their job was over.

"Oh, oh, that's great." She released Rye's hand and sat up, but he grasped her forearm, stopping her.

"Where do you think you're going?"

Darby squeaked in surprise not only from his words, but from his fierce hold. Her mouth parted in protest, however, a beep of Wyatt's phone cut her off.

Wyatt's brow furrowed. He appeared to show the same fortitude Rye displayed. "Hold that thought. I should see who that is just in case something is up." He reached into his pocket and pulled out his phone. He read a moment, threw his head back, and laughed boisterously.

Darby peeked at Rye in curiosity and discovered he stared at Wyatt with the same wonderment. She glanced back at Wyatt. "What is it?"

He looked away from the phone, still laughing. "We've just discovered the reason for all this." He said it more so to Rye than to Darby, but finally looked over at her and handed her the phone. "You've got to read this one for yourself."

She lay back down on the bed, resting her head on the pillow, and read the email aloud for Rye to hear.

As I'm sure you're all wondering, I had intended a month ago to pair the three of you up. I thought you'd make a lovely match together. Of course, Darby went missing. When it came to my attention, I used some sources to track her cell phone, which happened to be located at the house on Campbell Street. From what Darby told me of being distant with her family, I was concerned for her safety and that no one would know she was missing. I took it upon myself to look into this.

After sending one of my sources out, they discovered something was awry at the house. And this is how I knew of her location. I have heard you've apprehended Marcus Walsh and I'm pleased by such wonderful news.

I'm also happy to learn Darby is doing well and you have all reunited. Our agreement has now concluded, and I hope you've gotten everything you hoped for while using the 1Night Stand service.

Remember to always believe in a happily ever after.

Sincerely yours,
Madame Eve

Darby stared at the message, mouth agape. No, it couldn't be the Madame Eve she had hired to find her a man since she had no success with her own love life. Her gaze shifted from Wyatt to Rye. "Is this Madame Eve—the matchmaker?"

"That'd be the one," Rye replied.

Darby glanced between the men again, unable to wrap her head around how Madame Eve could pull this off. "You two hired her?"

"It's how we met," Wyatt answered. "I had originally hired her to pair me with a woman, but was matched with Rye a while back instead. Apparently, she still searched for the woman I had asked for. Clearly, from what I just read, you hired her, too."

"I did, but months ago." Darby's head spun. She shifted through the mess and a realization dawned on her. "What if I'd never hired Madame Eve? No one would have known I went missing until after my vacation was over." The horror of what could have happened hit her and stole her breath. "Oh my God, I could have."

CHAPTER SIX

W yatt placed his finger over her mouth, not wanting her to finish the thought. "But you didn't die. I can't begin to understand how Madame Eve does what she does, nor do I care. All I know is since the moment I met you, I had to watch over you, regardless of the fact I had no obligation to."

Her expression filled with surprise. "You didn't stay at my house because you were assigned to me?"

He shook his head. "It's not my job to keep anyone safe. It's my duty to find the criminal. But with you, I couldn't stay away."

"Why would you do that?" she whispered.

Wyatt glanced over her beautiful face. "There's a connection with you, Darby. I've tried to ignore it. Push past my want to keep you close. But I can't—and won't—deny it any longer."

"I'm beginning to understand exactly what you mean," Rye said, staring at her intently.

"No matter how strange the situation is," Wyatt continued. "Madame Eve has given Rye and I a helping hand and I won't doubt her. In fact, I didn't even need her to tell me she'd found our match because I knew it the day we met."

She stared at him, and for so long without saying a word. He glanced to Rye, who merely shrugged. He focused back on Darby. She blinked once before she grasped his face and kissed him.

Wyatt jumped away to fall ass first on the floor. "I didn't mean I wanted to rush things and be intimate with you."

Darby's eyes widened. She raised her hands to her mouth and said beneath them, "I. Can't. Believe. I. Just. Did. That."

Wyatt had no idea what to say to her. Luckily, Rye butted in. "Could be 'cause he has a sexy mouth."

Darby laughed, lowering her hands. "I've never done anything like that before—I'm sorry."

Rye sat up, settling in next to her. He took her chin. "Why *did* you do *that*?"

"I'm not sure. When Wyatt looked at me with those warm eyes of his, said those things, I just wanted to kiss him."

Wyatt shook his head to gather his thoughts. He hadn't expected that kiss, and he raised his fingers to his lips and swore she still lingered there. She might have initiated it because she lost control, but he struggled to maintain his position on the floor.

Rye studied her a moment longer. "You feel the connection, too, then?"

"I do," she whispered. "Even last night, there was a pull for me to be with you both. When I got into bed with you, nothing had ever been so right."

Rye's glanced over her face before he took her chin in his hand and pulled her face toward his. "May I kiss you, Darby?"

She simply nodded.

Wyatt's mouth dropped open with shock. Rye and Darby shared a very passionate kiss. He wanted to say something—do something. But he couldn't find his voice, only left to sit there like a fool on the floor.

Rye's mouth left hers, and he arched an eyebrow. "Something about this...about you...feels...."

"Right," Wyatt interjected. "No matter how wrong it is." He wanted all of her. He craved to take away what she'd been through, and he wanted to show her that even though Marcus tried to steal her life, she could gain it back.

He joined them on the bed and ran his thumb across her cheek. "I know the reaction I'm having to you and I know you've said you feel the same connection. But how do we know you aren't acting this way because of what you've been through? I don't want to take advantage of you."

Darby leaned against his hands, and her eyes closed for a moment. "I've never felt like I do with you two. Since you came to my house, I've never once felt the rising panic I've suffered lately, and that has to mean something. Even if this stirring is from what I've been through, because I need to be close to someone right now, it doesn't change the fact that this is what I want. Do I understand it all? No. Does it make sense?" She laughed, quietly. "Not at all. But being here with you two feels like it's exactly where I should be. For the first time since all this mess started, I'm happy."

Her lips invited him and wicked thoughts formed in Wyatt's mind, but he held his control. "I believe we should go at this slowly. No matter that Madame Eve has set this up, we don't need to rush anything. How about we get up and take you out for breakfast? Get to know you better."

She leaned in and her flowery scent filled Wyatt's nostrils. "I don't want breakfast. I don't want to leave this bed."

Rye chuckled. "Neither do I. I've had a stiffy all night from having you close, and I have no hesitation to go where your thoughts are headed."

Wyatt frowned at him. "Control yourself."

"I didn't offer the idea, but I'm damn well not going to refuse it," Rye said.

Darby laughed, sitting up.

Rye scooted toward her, but Wyatt held him back, focusing on Darby. "Are you sure this is what you want?"

"I'm not going to regret this, if that's what you're asking," she replied. "I'm twenty-seven years old; I think I can decide what I want. Besides, I've had casual lovers before. It's why I went to the bar that first night. I was looking for a little fun."

Her answer didn't resolve his hesitations. "Yes, but it's only been a month since you were attacked—"

She raised her hand, cutting him off. "Clearly, my desire to kiss you is an indicator of where my thoughts lay." She glanced at Rye before looking back at Wyatt. "My body needs this. I want the reminder of what it feels like to have a loving touch against my skin. I want to forget Marcus Walsh. I'm done with all that. I want to take back control of my life. I want to be happy again."

"And this will make you happy?" Wyatt asked.

"It's a start," was all she said.

He didn't need another invitation, because just like Rye, he'd been hard all night with her lying next to him. He released his hold on Rye, leaned in to press his lips against hers and moaned at first contact. It'd been some time since he kissed a woman, and he'd forgotten their softness. She pressed harder against his mouth, when suddenly a hand ran down the length of Wyatt's back. Rye's roughness told him so much, yet also showed he fought to be gentle, unleashing it on Wyatt's skin, not Darby's.

Rye removed his hand, and Wyatt continued to kiss her, opening his eyes to watch Rye trail his finger up her arm, displaying none of the tense moves Wyatt experienced from him. Darby shuddered. Her breath grew raspy. Her lips moved more forcefully with Wyatt's, commanding him to deepen his kiss. He'd not deny her.

He moved his mouth against hers, licking her bottom lip to allow him entrance, and she obliged him. Their tongues twined together. He groaned at her willingness to accept him.

The bed shifted and Rye knelt closer to her. Wyatt backed away and Rye removed her shirt. Her perky breasts greeted him, and Wyatt couldn't stop from gawking. Plump with dark nipples—the view delighted him. Yet, he caught sight of the scars along her body that would forever haunt her. His jaw clenched. Rye slid a finger down her neck and over the swell of her breast. Darby's eyes fluttered closed.

"Does that feel nice?" Rye whispered.

Her head fell back and she exhaled. "Yes."

Wyatt looked to Rye, to find a smoldering gaze staring back at him. Wyatt experienced the same desires.

As much as he wished he could reach out and offer Rye pleasure while they doted over Darby, he wanted to keep it all about her.

He focused back on her and touched along the curve of her breasts, hearing Darby sigh when he circled her nipple. Wyatt couldn't wait any longer. He leaned forward, followed by Rye, and licked along her flesh.

Darby latched onto Wyatt's head, held him firm while he sucked a nipple. Rye stayed a moment longer at her breasts before he started to lower his kisses. As he did, Wyatt helped Darby lie back down.

He shifted his face a little to still pay her nipple some attention, but he wanted to watch when Rye went down on her. Rye pulled her pajama pants off, and Wyatt's cock stiffened further seeing his lover's mouth against her. The way his tongue flicked out against her clit made him groan. The sight intrigued him enough. He wanted in on the fun.

He trailed his hand over Darby's thigh—her head was tilted back, her breasts high, her back arched. Wyatt continued to run his touch along her smooth skin until Rye backed away, allowing Wyatt to lean in. Even before he placed his mouth on her moist heat, he could smell her. It'd been so long since he had the musky scent of woman fill his nostrils. His cock was so needy; his only response was to unbutton his pants and lower his hand to stroke himself. But as he did, Rye removed his pants all together.

Clearly, Rye didn't hold the same concerns as Wyatt had. He might have voiced his hesitations if Rye hadn't taken him deep into his throat. Wyatt moaned against her flesh. Darby gasped, snapping her head up. Her gaze shifted from seeing Wyatt between her thighs to looking at Rye sucking him off. He wondered how she'd react to seeing them that way, but the desire in her wanton expression declared she wasn't put off by the idea. More so, she ground herself against Wyatt's face, earning a growl from him.

Rye grabbed Wyatt's cock, using his hand to follow the movements of his mouth. Wyatt reacted using more force against Darby's nub—he drew it between his teeth and sucked.

"Yes, oh God, yes...." Darby laced her fingers in his hair and gripped him tight.

Rye released Wyatt from his mouth, yet continued to stroke him. "Give it to him—let him see how good he's making you feel."

Darby trembled beneath his mouth, and Wyatt could barely focus since Rye stroked his cock with an unforgiving hand. He backed away, placing his fingers over her clitoris and rubbed with firm pressure.

She lifted her hips off the bed, squirming, but Wyatt never stopped. Not until she shuddered and lost herself in her release did he ease up, and not until she screamed a sound of pure pleasure did he kiss his way back up her body.

CHAPTER SEVEN

Darby's only focus was the men's lustful intentions. She finally found the strength to raise her head. Wyatt kissed his away along her torso. Rye continued to stroke him, and the sight of him touching Wyatt set her aflame. These two were the sexiest men she'd ever laid eyes on, and she quaked with desire at the sight of the burn in their eyes for not only each other, but her, too.

Rye released Wyatt's cock, jumped off the bed, and removed his boxers. Wyatt straightened up to stare at her. He rid himself of his shirt. Muscular physiques filled her vision, smooth tanned skin, toned in all the right places, and her gaze went lower to see both men had impressive cocks.

She watched Rye walk toward his luggage to see that tattoo of his ran down his back to his buttock. Her hunger soared—she'd never been so turned on by one man, let alone two.

"You're a lovely woman," Wyatt murmured, drawing her focus back to him. Making his way back up to her breasts, he caressed his cheek over her taut nipple. "I've not touched a woman in some time. The feel of your soft skin, the plushness of your breasts, and the sweet, tantalizing taste of you—it's doing wicked things to my body."

Darby opened her mouth to respond, but Wyatt turned his head again, placed his lips back over her nipple, and sucked. Nothing but a moan sounded from her throat. Her eyes fluttered closed.

Not until another set of hands ran up her arm did she open her eyes. Rye had returned and smiled at her, before handing Wyatt a condom. He didn't apply it and merely set it on the nightstand. She glanced down to see Rye had already sheathed the latex onto his erection. Her clit throbbed with the knowledge of what lay ahead.

Wyatt shifted away from her, and Rye moved in between her thighs and leaned in to kiss her. His kiss came more demanding while his fingers played with her sensitive flesh, only to stir desperation in her. When she ground her hips in time with his touches, Rye groaned with need before he pulled away, placed his cock at her entrance, and pushed in.

Darby's eyes rolled back into her head, and Rye made a noise suggesting it felt incredible to him, too. Wyatt petted her hair, and it drew her focus to him. He had placed one knee up on the bed to come close to her face.

He held his cock around the base and leaned in to place the tip at her mouth. Darby licked out, tasted the sweet, salty evidence of arousal there and drew it back into her mouth to savor it.

She raised her head up and Wyatt grabbed onto her neck. She drew him into her mouth. Wyatt's free hand came to her breast and he squeezed each breast, before he backed out slowly from her mouth. He rubbed his cock over Darby's lips. Rye thrust gently within her.

"What does she feel like, Rye?" Wyatt asked.

"Heaven." Rye groaned.

Darby opened her mouth for Wyatt to return where she wanted him. As Rye thrust within her pussy, Wyatt thrust into her mouth, and deep grunts from both men filled the space around her. She moaned, but Wyatt's cock settled deep into her mouth and cut off the sound.

Wyatt trailed his fingers down her body to reach her clit. With Rye moving in her, joined with Wyatt's attention along her nub, she was lost in pleasure. She released Wyatt from her mouth, grabbed him, and jerked his cock. "Oh God—that feels so good," she shouted, locked on Rye's molten gaze.

"Fuck, girl, you're so tight." Rye picked up speed, and Darby mirrored the move along Wyatt's cock. Wyatt leaned down to kiss her, and she twined her free hand into his hair to hold him close—her moans of pleasure captured by his hard, demanding kiss.

Rye grunted. Darby's pussy clamped around him, right before she soared into an all-consuming orgasm. Between her thighs, Rye tensed. He released a deep grunt, shuddered, and relaxed.

Wyatt never stopped kissing her. He switched positions with Rye, forcing her to release his cock. He backed away to apply the condom in haste then grabbed her hands. He pulled her up and lay down, so she straddled him with her hands resting on his chest. With Wyatt's smoldering gaze staring up at her, her arousal rose once again. He held himself ready and she sank down on him. She rocked her hips and Wyatt placed his hands under her bottom.

Rye reached down to take her chin and kissed her exactly the same way Wyatt had. Wyatt thrust upward, fast, but gentle. The pleasure captivated Darby. Rye ran his other hand along her face and caressed her with soft touches. She'd never felt so appreciated, so marveled over—the two men made her feel special.

Rye held her face in his hand, so close. He stared with eyes filled with emotion. "You're the prettiest damn thing I've ever seen." His gaze shifted to Wyatt. "Watching him with you is beautiful."

Wyatt moaned, never letting up on his thrusts, and Darby's eyes closed. Suddenly, the hold on her bottom left her, and Wyatt grasped her face, stealing her from Rye.

She opened her eyes to find a furrow between his eyebrows. Despite his serious look, intense emotion shone in his expression. He kept her face mere centimeters from his, his breath raspy on her face and so warm she shuddered, while he caged her in his grip. "Do you feel how crazy you are making me?"

She bit her lip, unable to speak, surprised Wyatt could. Her only response was a squeak when Rye flipped her hair over her shoulder and kissed her neck, her cheek, any area he could get his lips on.

Wyatt's grip tightened further, and possession rose in the depths of his eyes. "You're safe. You'll always be protected; that I promise you."

With his vow of protection, being held in the embrace of these two men who adored her, her pleasure rose. Rye captured her face again from Wyatt, angled her toward him, and drank in her moans with his mouth.

Wyatt grunted. Darby understood his reaction. He brought her to the edge of the cliff, too. He pumped, hard and fast. With a final cry, she surrendered. Her body tensed and pussy convulsed around his pulsating cock. She lost herself in the abyss of her orgasm, and he dove over the side with her.

By the time she returned to reality, she lay on her back, drenched in sweat while the two men cuddled in next to her. She looked between them. "So what happens now?" she asked, breathless.

"We see where this takes us." Wyatt smiled. "All that matters_"

"Is you're part of us now." Rye leaned up on his elbow to look down at Darby with a focused stare. "There's no denying there's something between us. Something special that none of us want to let go of, and we all know it. For me, and I can tell by the way Wyatt looks at you I'm not speaking alone, Madame Eve got this right. So, tell us, Darby, how will you fit into our relationship because we don't plan to let you go?"

Fate had worked itself in a strange way, but she wouldn't fight it or doubt it. Something did hold special between them that she couldn't quite explain, and something she didn't want to let go of either. They made love to her, touching her soul in ways she'd never experienced before, and that she never thought she'd experience again. Staring at them, she saw a shimmer of hope in their eyes. A want to know her and a desire for her to bring something to their lives they were missing.

"You know, I never imagined finding myself in a ménage relationship. But Madame Eve has worked a miracle, not only saving my life, but giving me another life to look forward to. I don't have to spend my whole life chasing what I used to be—trying to get my old life back—because now I can have something new." She glanced from Wyatt to Rye and smiled. "I'll fit somewhere in between."

Wyatt grinned. "In between the two of us_"

"Is the perfect place for you to be," Rye finished for him.

ALL SHE WANTS FOR CHRISTMAS IS HER DOM

BY

STACEY KENNEDY

CHAPTER ONE

The suite in the Castillo Lodge far exceeded Blake's expectations. Rustic in appearance with log walls, hardwood panel floors, and the rich scent of evergreens filling the air, it was exactly what he requested and fit the mood for a Christmas getaway. The room delighted him, but the woman who stood before him enchanted him more.

He led the blindfolded Taryn over to the four-poster wooden bed with a quilt on top and placed her hands on the railing over the footboard. "I suggest you present yourself." She bent over, spread her long, sexy legs, and angled her hips to expose her ass decorated by a thong. Her straight brown locks hung loosely down her back, covering the crimson lace bra that looked lovely against her pale skin. "Nicely done."

Her chest rose and fell quickly. *Nervous?* The thought only lingered on his mind a moment—no one paired with him would hold anxieties. As a Dom, he demanded much of his submissives. He needed them to be strong and obedient. And Madame Eve, a matchmaker out of Las Vegas who had arranged the encounter, had been well aware of that fact. As he examined her more closely, he equated her reaction to being aroused, and relished the thought that his mere presence caused her reaction.

"I'm here to please you, Sir."

The fire in the large stone fireplace on the far side of the large room cast a lovely glow over her skin. "Your desire to entice me is working." He pressed his hard cock against the seam of her ass to declare she hadn't been the only one affected. "I appreciate you addressing me with such respect, but for now, we can do without it. I'd advise, though, to use the term when you believe I want to hear it." He rubbed himself against her and held back his groan. "Is my cock what you want?"

"My pussy aches for you."

He chuckled before he moved away and saw her stance falter. "That kind of pleasure you'll have to earn."

She proved she was a skilled submissive as she recovered her position without pause. "I want to earn it, Sir."

He strode toward his bag on the floor by the stone fireplace and took out his flogger. She tensed as he flicked his hand to allow her to hear the sound of the tails whooshing through the air. "Do you have a safe word, my pet?"

"Marshal."

He positioned himself behind her and trailed the flogger over her backside. "Explain why that word holds significance?" He smacked her ass with a hard hit to test her limits.

"I'm a U.S. Marshal in Texas." She groaned. "Supervisory Deputy to be exact."

He ran the flogger over her bottom again to tease her. "Is that why the submissive role appeals to you, because of the job you hold?"

"It feels wonderful to give up the control I carry in my day-to-day life." She moaned as he issued another hit. "And I enjoy being punished."

He'd already known she enjoyed pain play. Madame Eve had sent him an extensive list of her limits, but he preferred learning for himself where those limits were drawn. "How long have you lived the BDSM lifestyle?"

"Five years." She squeaked as he delivered a hard hit on her back then let the tails of the flogger tickle down the sweet cheeks of her ass.

"But you haven't had a lifestyle Dom?"

"I—" She paused. "I'd prefer not to discuss it."

Unacceptable. He hit hard twice. She bowed her head and cringed. "I didn't ask what you preferred. Answer the question."

She breathed deep as he hit lightly along her thighs. "I did have someone, but not anymore."

"Would he be jealous that I'm your Dom tonight?"

"I'd imagine he would be." She gasped when he flogged her on the shoulders and continued down her back.

"I suppose then, I'll need to leave my mark on you for all to see, so they're well aware who you belong to now." He hit harder.

Her flesh turned a lovely shade of red, but he knew she could take more. He needed to up the intensity and push her further. "Reach into your panties and rub your clit. But if you orgasm without permission you will displease me. Am I understood?"

"Yes, Sir." She lowered her hand into her thong and moaned as she played with her clit.

He raised the flogger and slapped her again, repeatedly moving his arm in a figure-eight pattern. Her skin burned red as he whipped her without mercy. She cringed, complained with yelps, but he suspected she enjoyed every damn minute of it.

She impressed him. Her control, ability to handle pain, and desire to please him had been honorable. That is, until he caught sight of something that tightened his jaw. Her body trembled but not in a way that informed him the pain had been too intense. No, she had defied him.

He hit her twice and meant the strokes to hurt. "Did you orgasm?"

"I'm sorry, Sir." She panted.

He gripped her hair and pulled back to expose her face. The blindfold had not moved. Her parted lips trembled as she sucked in deep breaths and her cheeks were as red as her ass. "You did not answer my question."

"It's been so long since I've been flogged. It felt incredible. I couldn't help myself, Sir."

He *tsked*. "If you had asked permission, I would have granted you the right. Now, though, you will need to earn back such luxuries and be punished for your mistake." He approached his bag again where he grabbed out two five-pound weights and his whip. "Raise your arms to shoulder height and do *not* lower them."

She complied and he placed the weights in her hands. "Turn slowly in a circle and keep those weights high."

He took a step back then sent the whip to connect with her torso, flicking his wrist in time with her spin so with each turn she made, the whip connected with a new area on her body. She sucked in a breath and flinched away.

Red marks decorated her skin. Her moans, mixed with pleasure and pain, drifted over to caress him like a warm hand stroking his cock. He continued until her arms shook from exhaustion and he'd marked her body beautifully. "You will not orgasm again without permission. Do I make myself clear?"

"Yes, Sir." Her legs trembled and her voice shook. "My arms are hurting, Sir. May I lower them?"

She'd been punished, which was his intention—to make sure

she never disobeyed him again—but he'd not let her off that easy. She had asked for his punishment to end instead of him granting it. She had defied him again. "You're inability to do as I ask is disappointing."

"I don't mean to fail you, Sir."

"I'm finding that hard to believe since you continually do so." He took the weights from her, tossed them aside, and massaged her arms. "If such were the case I would find myself rewarding you more than I am punishing."

Taryn's Dom rubbed her arms and relieved the soreness. His procedure of punishment seemed so familiar. Her ex-boyfriend punished that hard and always made her work for her reward. She shook the thought from her mind. Past lovers should have no place in her mind now.

She wanted to look at him, but he hadn't allowed her to remove the blindfold. When she agreed in her questionnaire to Madame Eve that she'd been comfortable with the idea of shielding her eyes, she had assumed it had been the way he wanted her to be presented to him. She had not expected she'd be blindfolded the entire time—never to see him at all.

He released her arms, and she listened as he strode to the other side of the room. Her heart raced for what was to come next. She held no doubt he would make an example of her failures. Part of her welcomed the pain she expected would be soon upon her. The other part was fearful of his harsh punishments.

His presence returned a moment later. Even though she couldn't see him, his energy simmered around her and her mind played with images of what he looked like. Tall, dark, and handsome with a body that made her damp between her thighs—or so she hoped.

"Lower to your hands and knees."

She obeyed and positioned herself on all fours, and did her best to make the pose as sexy as possible to entice him.

He tapped her back and she recognized the feel of a cane. The burn that followed the hit was undisputable. "Do you want to earn back how much you've disappointed me?"

"With all that I am, Sir." It had been years since she'd been in the submissive role, and anger at herself for not having more control set in. She wanted him to acknowledge her as submissive, be proud of what she accomplished, and even more so, wanted the reward of a job well done.

"Well then, my pet, you'll take what I'm going to give you with little argument. Am I understood?"

"Yes, Sir."

He struck her lightly between the shoulder blades, but even a gentle tap with a cane was painful. She dipped her head and breathed deeply. She'd learned the skill long ago to bottle the pain and convert it into something brilliant—use it to bring herself to a higher level of arousal.

The hits continued to travel along her torso, to her bottom, and travelled down to the back of her thighs until the cane met the arch of her foot. She hissed but didn't dare voice her pain with words. No, she needed to please him, for him to stop punishing her, and be in awe of her submissiveness.

"Reach your hand out." She did and he placed a bullet vibrator in her palm. "Find a way to turn it on, then lower your head down to the floor and place it against your clit."

She fumbled as she attempted to find the on button—she eventually did—then placed her cheek against the hard floor and arched her back. She positioned the vibrator into her panties and the buzz along her clit made her eyes roll back into her head.

"I will not have to remind you of what you must ask for, will I?"

She forced herself to draw away from her pleasure and find her voice to answer him. "No, Sir. I will not come without permission."

She heard the sound of the cane swoosh through the air before the hard wood hit her bottom. She nearly cried out, but swallowed it back. He walloped her with such force she suspected welts would be a reminder of tonight.

Not that she minded. She deserved the punishment—enjoyed the treatment he gave her—and she sucked in the pain with each breath. She pushed the vibrator harder against her clit in a demand that her body ignore the sharp sting.

He placed his foot between her shoulder blades to pin her and continued with hard smacks against her sore flesh. She worked the vibe feverishly against her clit to offset the agony. Yet, as he spanked her ass in between the torment of the cane, she couldn't hold back.

She screamed as heat burned through her body. The increase of pain introduced the rise of her climax. The sensation stole all of her reason and overloaded her nerve endings with pleasure. "May I come, Sir?"

He removed his foot, placed his hand on her nape, and caged her in his grip. "You may. But you damn well better make it impressive." He slapped along her body—from her neck all the way to her sore ass—and never missed a piece of her tender flesh.

His hits stung, but they held no comparison to the overwhelming surge of pleasure erupting in her body. Her clit pulsed, pussy contracted, and she vocalized her pleasure to allow him to hear the intensity of her orgasm. She had not come so hard in years and she lost herself completely with the force of it.

It hadn't been until his finger trailed down her arm did she return from the blissful place she'd been sent to. "Stand, but take it slow." He helped her up, steadied her, and even supported her for a while. "Are you feeling light-headed at all?"

She groaned as the world spun around her. Her heartbeat raced and a cold sweat washed over her body. She exhaled slow and steady, and waited for her body to recover from his harsh treatment.

Many minutes later, her feet felt more stable on the floor and her body no longer tingled. "I'm feeling better now." He pushed on her slightly and her bottom connected with a cold, smooth surface—the log wall she assumed—and the coolness against her sore rump came as a relief.

"Don't move." He released his hold on her arm, and she heard shuffling before he closed back in on her. She worried for a moment that he might issue more pain, but when he pulled her from the wall and applied cool cream along her bottom, she sighed. The smooth lotion eased the sting on her skin and soothed her. Still, she doubted she'd sit right for a week.

He used a gentle touch as he tended to her. She flinched a few times at the marks that had clearly been the worst, but felt more relaxed than she had in a long time. There, she found her peace. It wasn't spa days, or therapy sessions—this was where she could release all of her strain. Euphoria filled her soul.

He covered her whole body with the cream, finished up at her ankles and stood. She heard him move in front of her while he rubbed the remaining lotion into his hands. Each breath she took only seemed to draw out the moment of complete silence.

"You've done well tonight."

He trailed a finger down her cheek, and being already

sensitive, she shivered. More so, the pride sounding in his voice brought forth emotions long hidden. She'd withstood all his punishment and she'd done right by him. Her self-confidence rose to a level it hadn't been at in years.

"Thank you, Sir."

"You're quite welcome."

His voice wavered in such a way that made her hesitate, and the sound drained all of her pride and happiness. "Sir, why does it sound as if our night is over?"

"Because, my pet, it is."

"But I've taken your punishment." She paused. Yes, he'd rewarded her with a climax, but she had yet to have him. She wanted his cock and the ache in her pussy declared she needed him. "What have I done to displease you, Sir?"

"No more formalities, please."

"What have I done then? Tell me what I did to upset you that you will not offer yourself to me?" Tears rimmed her eyes behind the mask. She'd been taken on a high, soared along the fantastic ride, only to be dropped with no net.

He took her hand and squeezed. "You've done nothing wrong. In fact, you did everything right." His voice sounded so different than it had this whole time—almost unsure.

It unsettled her. Before she had a chance to ask him more, he released a low deep breath. "Remove the blindfold, Taryn."

She blinked beneath it and tried to process what she'd heard. Up to that point, her Dom had not said her name and the sound of it hit her with a memory.

It can't be.

She yanked the blindfold down, so she could laugh at herself for thinking that this man just then sounded so much like her ex-boyfriend. But as her vision adjusted from being held in the dark for so long, warm hazel eyes greeted her, along with a charming smile.

"Blake?"

He grinned. "Surprised to see me?"

CHAPTER TWO

Blake had no preconceived notion about how Taryn would react, and had been surprised she hadn't recognized his voice, even though he tried his best to disguise it. He didn't want her to know who mastered her because he wanted to remind her of what he had to offer. Now, he merely let the seconds tick by until she had resolved her thoughts.

She finally blinked, but still stared blank-faced at him. "How can this be?"

"Madame Eve contacted me three weeks ago—as I'm sure she did you—and invited me to the Christmas celebration here at the lodge to meet my match, and also extended an invitation to attend the gala on Christmas Day. It's my hope that you'll join me."

She shook her head as if she were unable to process what he told her. "Are you telling me we met again by chance?"

"No." The Christmas Eve encounter had taken not only planning by Madame Eve, but he'd had to make life changes in order to be the man he needed to be when he saw Taryn again.

"Then, what?" Her confused expression shifted to a scowl.

"You set this up? You knew you were meeting me tonight and said nothing?"

"You agreed to keep our identities a secret until tonight," he gently reminded her. "Madame Eve must have thought it was appropriate that I knew we were being matched, but she didn't disapprove of my wanting to surprise you."

"That means nothing—who cares what Madame Eve thinks? *You* should have told me." She glared. "I cannot believe you did this." She strode over to her suitcase, grabbed a pair of pants, plus a shirt, and set about getting dressed. "You should have warned me. Told me it was you. You had no right to assume I even wanted to be with you again." She never looked back, but he could tell by her curt tone that she loathed him.

She dressed and he saw her wince as the clothing settled over her sore body. He wanted to help, but knew better than to approach her right then. He leaned against the wall, crossed his arms, and waited for her to calm down. The Taryn in front of him was one he knew well. If he said a word, she'd trap him in an impossible situation he'd never recover from—nothing he did would ease her. He waited for her to stop being so angry, to allow herself time to think.

"And there you go—like you always did—saying nothing while I'm the only one letting my feelings be known." She scowled at him. "You have nothing to say?"

He shook his head. *Not right now. Not when you've cornered me.*

Her eyes narrowed, her face turned a dark shade of red, and rage wafted off her. "I'm so fucking angry with you." She spun on her heels, heading for the patio door, only dressed in the T-shirt and a pair of jeans. "Go home."

He sighed, annoyed, infuriated, and frustrated. He hoped she'd be more receptive to him—that she missed and wanted him as much as he did her—but her demand had been firm. She wanted nothing to do with him.

It only confirmed he had made the right choice in how he approached her. If he had knocked on her door or even called her, she would have run—just like she did now. He wanted to show her the spark that existed between them, and he held no doubt she'd witnessed it tonight. He suspected her hesitation came from the night he broke her heart and she broke his—too swamped with old pain to see straight.

He had lived that life for the past five years, and he wouldn't walk in the shadow of despair any longer. He hadn't gone through all he had to ensure this night happened to let her walk out of his life again.

Fuck this. She's mine.

He snatched the quilt off the bed and strode out after her. The snowy mountains of Alaska stood picturesque against the moonlight sky. The ski hill was lit up and he could hear laughter as guests enjoyed the cold winter's night. His focus remained on finding Taryn. Each step he took into the deep snow froze his feet as the icy air made him shiver.

He passed a large snowdrift, and she appeared standing beside an evergreen tree. Her head was in her hands and she sobbed. He sighed in relief. Her first reaction might have been anger, but as always, she'd break down and let him in.

He stepped in behind her, placed the quilt over her shoulders, and turned her to face him. It tugged at his heart seeing the pain in the depths of her eyes—pain he'd put there. "Are you ready to talk now?"

"I wasn't expecting this," she said so softly he barely heard her. "Why wouldn't you tell me it was you?"

"Because I wanted to remind you of how good we are together before you knew that I was with you. I didn't want you to react exactly like you did."

Her eyes narrowed but there was no heat in her gaze. "How else was I supposed to act? You blindsided me and violated the trust."

"I did nothing you didn't agree to. Madame Eve told you exactly what would take place here. You knew you'd be blindfolded, brought into a BDSM scene, and you agreed to know nothing about me before tonight. You, not me, set the limits. I merely followed them." He cocked his head. "Did you not question why I never engaged you sexually?"

"You...." He saw the argument rise on her expression before she stopped herself. "You're right. You made me pleasure myself and never touched me in that way."

"Nor did I kiss you. I acted as your Dom and nothing more, which had all been things you agreed to. In fact, you wanted sex if I remember and didn't I refuse you? I might have gone about this in a way you disprove of, but I would not have taken you without you knowing the truth."

She studied him—the sadness, dismay, and even the anger dissipated from her face—she looked exhausted. "How did Madame Eve know about us? How did she arrange this?"

"I hired Madame Eve four months ago, filled out the questionnaire in search of a lifestyle submissive, and as you know she asked about previous relationships."

"So you told her about me?"

He brushed his knuckles across her cheek and it pleased him when she leaned into his touch. "Of course I would."

"But...." Her chin quivered. "But I don't understand. You let me go."

He deserved to see how much his actions hurt her, and she hid none of it in her expression. "What was I to do? You came to me and spoke of big dreams in Houston."

"You could have come with me."

A tear fell down her cheek and he caught it with his thumb. "I couldn't and you know that. I had the contract to build the new library in Sackville. I would have lost the deal and that project made the company what it is today."

"You lost me."

His heart clenched. The truth hurt. "A bad decision on my part, but not one I'll make again." It took a good part of the last two weeks to organize his life and get his priorities straight. But he'd not live another day in a life he didn't want and be away from the woman who fulfilled him. "I sold the business a week ago and moved to Houston last weekend."

Her eyes went huge. "You sold the business...for me?"

"It's always been you, Taryn, and *will* always be you. It hadn't been until Madame Eve contacted me and told me you had signed up with her services, did I realize I couldn't live another day without you. I saw that I had submerged myself in my work to try to forget you but that I failed miserably—all that remained was an empty man."

"Blake," she whispered.

He needed to explain himself and pressed on to share his soul with her. "Madame Eve felt regardless of what happened between us, that we were a perfect match and I happened to agree with her." He leaned in and her warm breath tickled his lips as the crisp air nipped at his skin. "I've made enough money. Yes, I could make more, but without you I have nothing."

She exhaled so deep the air fogged around them. "I have waited five years for you to say what you just said to me. There has not been a day where I haven't thought of you, missed being in your arms, and craved to be your submissive. If I wasn't as cold as I am now, I'd think I was dreaming, but I doubt I'd feel frostbitten in a dream."

He chuckled. "Best we warm you up then." He gathered her in

his arms, trudging through the snow with one intent—spend the rest of the night reminding himself and her how right it was for them to be together.

♐

Taryn welcomed the warm air from the suite as Blake shut the sliding door. He turned back to her, his eyes intent and her insides melted. She dropped the blanket to the floor as he latched onto her arms and yanked her toward him. He placed his lips over hers and set to make her forget her own name.

She swiped her tongue across his as he kissed her deeply. It'd been so long since she had his lips on hers, she'd forgotten how good the man could kiss. No one kissed her with the fevered pitch that he did, and no one but him could make her legs wobble.

He backed away, only a moment, and removed his shirt. She ran her hands over his chest, down his toned abs, and was delighted when they clenched beneath her touch. He'd always been muscular, but not like this. Her pussy ached for him at the feel of each groove beneath her fingers.

He left her mouth, to kiss along her jaw, to her shoulder where he bit. She gasped, but the throb along her clit only pulsed deeper. He touched her just how she liked it—rough and never hesitated. It made her burn. She raised her arms when he grabbed her shirt and lifted it over her head. He wasted no time removing her bra, pants, and panties then stepped back to examine her.

"I want you to know that it had been a torment not to see you naked—not to be able to touch your splendid pussy." He cupped her moist heat and squeezed tight. She ground herself against his hand. "Fuck, Taryn, you're a sexy woman."

The crackling fire lit his face in a warm glimmer. *My Blake. My Dom.* She'd missed him terribly, and seeing him like this, so powerful in front of her—she wondered how she'd gone so long without him. She had mourned their break-up for the past five years and her heart welcomed the healing.

He must have seen the happiness in her expression because he smiled. "We could exchange sentiments, but I'd much prefer to let your body speak to how happy you are that I'm here with you now." He gestured to his pants. "Remind me of what I've been missing these past five years."

She sank to her knees, kept her gaze focused on his, and undid his belt. His eyes burned with a wicked light and butterflies danced in her stomach. His black slacks pooled at his feet as his heavy cock rested at eye-level. She ran her hands up his thighs, licked the tip of his dick, and savored the salty liquid on her tongue.

He threaded his fingers through her hair and stared hungrily at her. She kissed his thighs, ran her tongue along his muscular legs, and trailed her hands along his abs. He tensed as she blew lightly on his cock and then slid her tongue up his shaft in a firm stroke. She brought him into her mouth and took him deep into her throat.

She backed away not a moment later and moistened him with her saliva before wrapping her hand around his erection to spread the warm liquid along his cock. She flicked the tip with her tongue to tease him, drew in a long breath, then went wild on him.

His hand tightened in her hair as she bobbed her head while she stroked his cock without mercy. His moans washed along her skin, raising goose bumps, as his cock hardened even more against her tongue. Each sound he made urged her to suck harder, stroke faster, and within only minutes, he jumped away from her.

"That...." He sounded breathless. "That was one hell of a good reminder." He leaned down to cage her face in his hands and took her mouth with a hard kiss that dampened her pussy.

He broke off the kiss, and she gasped at the loss of contact.

"Nothing pleases me more than having the scent of my cock on your mouth."

Her clit pulsed at the low growl of possession in his tone.

"You are to remain kneeling there." He approached a bag on the floor and took a large square black velvet box. He turned back to her and smiled. "I got you something."

She took the box from him and ran her hand over the rich fabric. "What did you do?"

"Go on." He gestured toward the box. "Open it."

She glanced back to the gift, opened the lid, and gasped when sparking diamonds greeted her. "Oh, Blake...."

"Stand and let me decorate you."

He took the jewelry out of the box and it appeared to be a long necklace. She stood, turned her back to him, and he flicked her hair across her shoulder. "This, my pet, will be what I expect you to wear when we are in a scene together—a statement that my diamonds are along your skin and the knowledge that you are worthy of wearing such treasures."

Her breath hitched as he tightened the choker around her throat. The statement he made brought tears to her eyes. She ran her fingers along the choker, down the two rows of diamonds between her breasts and continued until she hit the belly chain as he fastened it. Nothing had ever felt so right.

He turned her to face him and his eyes shone with adoration. "You look perfect, exactly as you should, and now you understand what this symbolizes."

A marriage proposal meant something to some people, but in her world, this meant so much more. "You've collared me and claimed me as yours."

His powerful gaze burned scorching heat through her body reaching down to her center. "Yes, my pet, I've collared you, but I haven't claimed you—not completely, anyway."

CHAPTER THREE

The diamonds enhanced Taryn's beauty, and Blake would never grow tired of looking at her. She'd been marked as his and had accepted him as her lifestyle Dom. But his needy cock reminded him to stop admiring her and claim her.

He approached his bag and took out the last of the items he'd brought—four pieces of long black rope. Her breath hitched as he returned to her, confirming she still enjoyed the feel of restraints. He took her hand, led her in front of the footboard then turned her around so her ass rested against the wood, and she faced him. If he could have placed her on the bed, tied her down and done the wicked things he wanted to, he would have. But her body would be sore from the punishment earlier and her wellbeing stayed on his mind.

He sank to his knees, took one of her ankles, and tied the rope tight against her skin. He attached the remaining rope to the post on the bed before he repeated the move on the other ankle, and then did the same to her wrists to leave her caged between the posts on the bed.

His cock ached to slam into her slick pussy, but he'd not stray from what he'd craved for years. "Every day since you were gone, I thought of how you taste and your sweet honey tormented me." He licked out to savor her and groaned as her cream delighted his tongue. "Exactly as I remembered."

He smacked her pussy and hit her clit hard. "I grant you the right to not address me as Sir as long as you tell me nothing but the truth. Tell me how much you want my cock?"

"I've thought of your cock every time I masturbated. I've dreamed of how it used to fill me up, and I want you to make me come like you always could."

He took her clit between his fingers and pinched. "While you fucked yourself, what did you think of?"

"I-I...." She moaned. "I thought of how you used to make me feel. The way your power would wash over me, just like it did tonight, and how I'd do anything I could to please you."

He inserted a finger inside of her, then another, and her pussy tightened around him. "Did you do this while you thought of me?"

"Yes, always."

He grasped her hip and he thrust his fingers inside of her with a steady rhythm. His muscles burned as he fingered her, and she bucked under his touch. He flicked her clit with his tongue and she shook, indicating a rising climax, but he wanted his mouth to offer her orgasm, not his fingers. He withdrew them, slid his tongue into her moist heat, and she hissed as she stared at him. Her hooded eyes made his cock stiffen further. He grabbed it and stroked himself.

The sight clearly pleased her since her eyes darkened as she watched him jerk off. He used his free hand to pinch her clit again and her moans encouraged him. He increased his speed with his tongue until her breath froze, her eyes widened, and her body quivered—all followed by a whoosh of air from her, indicating she was in the throes of her orgasm.

He swirled his tongue and her body trembled against his lips. He gave her a final, deep lick all the way up until he reached her clit then kissed it. He sat back on his legs and ran his fingers lightly over his shaft, while he waited for her to acknowledge his presence again.

&#x0x25B;

The haze cleared from Taryn's vision and she watched Blake as he touched himself in a way to make her spent body awaken. "I'm not the only one who is incredible with their mouth."

He winked as he stood, and then approached his pants on the floor. He took out a condom from his wallet, applied the latex over his rock hard cock, and then looked back to her. His gaze looked nothing less than a man who planned to fuck her savagely and, she eagerly awaited him.

He returned to her, gripped her hip, and placed his cock against her slick entrance. "Are you ready for me, my pet?" She nodded and he pushed in. She groaned—a sound he mirrored. "You're fucking tight."

"I should be." She gasped. "I haven't had sex with anyone since you."

"Nor have I."

The acknowledgment he'd not been with another made her blissfully happy, but she was too lost in the pressure along her pussy. She watched as he rubbed his cock along her heat and tweaked her clit. She shifted her pelvis forward and circled her hips in time with his touch. Her moves inched him into her tight pussy, but slowly. He allowed her to take him in and his only help had been when he stepped forward so she could wiggle her way onto him.

By the time he was fully seated inside her, her pussy released to accept him, and his thick cock stretched her in a beautiful way. He grabbed her hips with both hands, placed his forehead against hers, and closed his eyes.

"I've craved to be right here for so long." He dipped lower and fucked her in the exact way she liked it—hard and ruthless. Each thrust made her moan, squirm, and made her pussy so wet.

He withdrew his cock, dragged his arousal over her anus, and then rejoined her. He grabbed onto her bottom, gave it a tight squeeze before he dipped his hand between her cheeks and inserted a finger into her tight bud.

She gasped at the initial intrusion, but pleasure immediately followed, flooding her with sensations. He continued to thrust in her pussy with primal strokes that had her struggling against the bonds.

He lowered his head to bite the sweet spot along her neck and she cried out. The burn along her skin, paired with the pressure in her pussy awakened her climax. But just as her body hinted at a release, he withdrew his cock.

"Don't stop."

He grinned haughtily. "You don't think I'd let you come that easily, do you?"

She should have known better. His finger in her bottom moved and it awakened a new sense of pleasure for her. Her clit and her pussy ached for him to return but as he denied it, only to offer it somewhere else, it stole her breath.

"I know your pussy hasn't been fucked, but has your ass?" He continued to stroke the tight knot. "Has anyone used your ass like I used to?"

"No," she barely managed.

"This shall be a real treat for me then." He removed his

finger and strode back over to his bag. He took out a bottle of lube, and her body scorched in need of him. He applied a new condom before he spread the clear liquid to his cock and coated it. He dipped some onto his fingers and threw the bottle to the ground.

He returned to her and ran his fingers over her ass, and inserted his finger to ready her. She moaned, but he drank in her sounds as he took her mouth so rough she could barely keep up. He loosened the binds on her ankles, then grabbed her hips to angle them forward, which tightened the ropes around her wrists but she welcomed the burn.

Whenever he got rough in his kisses, it meant his end was near and that meant he'd fuck her senseless. He smacked his cock against her clit, and already being aroused, she gasped against the intense sensation. He ran the tip of his dick down her pussy and pulled her hips out further to gain access to her. The rope dug into her wrists, but as he reached her anus, she forgot the pain and he gave a steady push.

She hissed at the pressure, but did her best to relax. Gripping her hips, he angled her more toward him and pushed in deeper. He leaned in to kiss her again as his cock passed through the tight rim. Running his hand along her stomach to her clit, where he circled the little nub, he started to thrust in and out of her with ease.

Her eyes widened as a rush of erotic fulfillment titillated her senses. Her wrists burned from the hold, the pressure built along her ass, and her pussy ached for his cock but all the opposing sensations spiked her climax.

"Fuck, woman, I love every damn thing about you." He all but growled. His skin smacked against her as her pleasure skyrocketed.

"I love you, too," she shouted. "Make me come with you."

"Yes, sweetheart, come for me." He backed his chest away, dipped even lower, and pushed his fingers into her pussy.

She lost her breath—immediately consumed with a rich source of energy. Everything else disappeared as he finger-fucked her while his cock pounded her ass. Her head fell back, eyes shut tight, and she screamed against the pressure building inside of her. Her body had been overwhelmed with some pain and some pleasure—all of it extraordinarily fantastic.

Every muscle tightened as though a bomb went off in her center. A rush of pure and unadulterated pleasure awakened every nerve. He thrust in an unforgiving way until he buried himself deep and roared out his satisfaction.

She returned to the present when he withdrew. Her body felt used—sore in all the right places, and in other places that might have been wrong to some. He made quick work to rid her of the ropes and her muscles held no strength, but before she could slump to the floor, he had her in his arms.

She glanced at him and his warm, powerful gaze stared back at her. She hadn't expected any of this to happen but Madame Eve had been right—they were a perfect match. She might have told herself she'd gotten over him and that her career stood above all else, but it had all been a lie.

Blake adored her in a way no one else dared to and treated her exactly how she wanted to be treated. He knew all her deepest, darkest desires, and he didn't run from her fantasies, but fulfilled them. "I'll never leave you again."

He smiled and kissed her lips in a gentle way that showed how complex a man he really was. "And I'll never let you go."

~ABOUT THE AUTHOR~

Stacey Kennedy's urban fantasy/paranormal and erotic romance series have hit Amazon Kindle and All Romance Ebooks Bestseller lists. If she isn't plugging away at her next novel, tending to her two little ones, she's got her nose deep in a good book. She lives in Ontario, Canada with her husband.

Be sure to drop her a line at www.staceykennedy.com, she loves to hear from her readers.

Immerse yourself in fantasy with stories of love and lust from

Decadent Publishing

www.decadentpublishing.com